OTHER TITLES FROM
DIAMONDSTONE PRODUCTIONS

PICKET FENCES BY: WADE
THE FACTOR BY: FACE
HALFWAY CROOKZ BY: $PAID
DAMAGED GOODS BY: NIKKI URBAN
JADE'S DIARY BY: NIKKI URBAN

COMING SOON FROM
DIAMONDSTONE PRODUCTIONS

THE PERSONAL TRILOGY BY: WADE

PERSONAL 1
PERSONAL 2
PERSONAL 3

DiamondStone Productions, LLC
PO Box 11266
Jacksonville, FL 32239-11266
Diamondstoneproductions.net
Printed in the United States of America

Edited By: Melissa Bennett
Cover: Jarvis Traylor
Model: London Jackson

Kontagious

NIKKI URBAN

PROLOGUE

Kandice picked up her Fendi purse, car keys, and Fendi shades, and walked out of the store, closing it down for the rest of the day. The ride to the hospital was nerve-racking for her. She called Derrick before she pulled out of the parking lot, telling him to meet her at the hospital. Fifteen minutes later Kandice was parking her car in the hospital's parking garage and racing into Virgie's room.

When she walked into the room Kandice saw the doctor talking to Derrick. She walked up to them just as Virgie started to have a seizure and her body began to shake uncontrollably. The doctor rushed over to her bed while the nurses rushed inside the room.

The nurses told Kandice and Derrick that they had to leave, but neither one of them moved toward the door. Derrick gave the nurses a death stare, letting them know that he would lay hands on them if they expected him to leave Virgie's side.

As suddenly as the seizure started, it stopped.

"What the hell just happened to her?" Derrick shouted as he walked to Virgie's bedside and grabbed her hand. He could not contain the tears that began running down his cheeks. Derrick could not stand to see his Virgie in this condition. He felt helpless and he would be devastated if God took her from him.

Virgie squeezed his hand and stared deep into his eyes. She opened her mouth to speak to him before she took her last breath. "D... errick," Virgie said in a weak voice.

Derrick cried harder as he watched the woman who had raised him gasping for air. "My Virgie, don't talk. I need you to save your energy," Derrick pleaded as he stared back into her eyes.

Virgie paid him no attention and tried again to talk. She swallowed her saliva and tried again to say what *was on her heart.* *"Baby... ummm."*

Virgie never finished her sentence, because the hospital equipment that she was hooked up to began to beep loudly, signaling that her heartbeat was dropping. Dr. Davis heard the machine and rushed to Virgie's side, pushing Derrick out of his way. The alarm from the machine sent an emergency notification to the nurses' station and several more nurses rushed into the room. Two of the nurses had to physically force Derrick and

Kandice out of the room as the medical staff tried to save Virgie's life.

Reluctantly, Derrick and Kandice walked into the hall. Derrick was losing his mind. He began to swing his arms wildly in the air as he poured out his grief from within the depths of his being. Kandice also became emotional as she watched her husband. She quickly grabbed him and embraced him.

Derrick grabbed his wife's body and held on for dear life. He cried and she just held him, trying to bring him some comfort. As they continued to embrace, the door to Virgie's door opened and Dr. Davis stood there silently. The look on the doctor's face spoke volumes.

Before Dr. Davis could even tell them that Virgie had died, Derrick fell to his knees and wept like a newborn baby. Dr. Davis helped Kandice pull Derrick off the floor.

"You can go in there and say your goodbyes," he said softly. "I'm sorry I couldn't save her."

Derrick and Kandice walked back inside the room. They were both quiet as they noted how peaceful Virgie now looked. Derrick touched her face and caressed her long, silver hair. After a few more moments of silence he was able to compose himself enough to profess his love for her and to tell her that a piece of him had died with her.

Kandice remained quiet and allowed her husband to have his time with his mother. She said a silent prayer, asking God to give them the strength to endure this time of grief and help them to remain strong for each other. Although Virgie and Kandice were never that close, they both had a mutual respect for the other, and they shared a deep love for Derrick. Kandice looked at Virgie's face and said her final goodbye, silently praying that God would welcome her home. Then her mind drifted to what Virgie might have been trying to tell Derrick right before she'd passed.

Derrick stood in front of the casket as it was lowered into the ground. He could not bring himself to shed another tear. He was all cried out. He had lost the one woman whom he'd loved unconditionally—his mother. His Virgie-Mae was going home to be amongst God's angels.

Kandice watched from a distance as she saw her husband mourn the loss of his mother. She felt helpless, because she was unsure as to how to console him. As she watched Derrick from the sideline, she felt a pair of eyes watching her. Instead of looking to see who was watching, she simply pulled her fur coat closer to her body and strutted over to her husband.

Whoever's watching me can watch me switch my ass and catch a whiff of this sweet pussy," she thought.

The two of them stood side by side without saying a word. Kandice placed her hand inside Derrick's hand and they watched the ditch diggers shovel the dirt onto Virgie's casket. She felt him squeeze her hand slightly. She turned and looked at her husband and saw silent tears falling down his cheeks. Kandice embraced him and cradled him close to her heart. She was heartbroken when she saw that her husband was so distraught.

Derrick composed himself. He knew that Virgie-Mae would not have wanted him to break down like this, but instead to be strong.

"I'm fine, Ma," he whispered. "I just wanted to say goodbye one last time, ya know. Let's go," he said to Kandice as he turned to walk away. The ride in the limo back to the house was a short one, but it seemed like an eternity for Derrick. He always knew that this day would come, but his heart was unprepared for it.

The house was packed with people who had come to pay their respects to Virgie-Mae. When Derrick and Kandice entered their home they were greeted with many hugs, kisses, pats on the backs, condolences, and cards.

Derrick made his way to the bar in the den and poured himself a glass of Hennessy Richard cognac. Then he walked to the window that overlooked the man-made lake that sat at the back of his home. Soon he felt the presence of company gracing his side. A smile crept across his lips as he thought back to the first time that the two of them had met.

1990... 16th Birthday

"All right, lil man, you ready for your surprise!" Virgil asked Derrick as he pulled away from the curb.

Derrick was so amped for his sixteenth birthday that he didn't even ask what his gift was. He just hoped it was something that he was going to like.

Thirty minutes later they were pulling up to the Hyatt Regency right outside the city's limits.

Virgil pulled out a room key with a number written on it and handed it to Derrick. Derrick looked oddly at Virgil and the key before he accepted it.

"What's up with this?" he asked.

"This is your gift. When you get inside you will see what I mean. A limo will be here to pick you up tomorrow morning. I already talked with Virgie-Mae, and she's cool. I told her that you were going to be with me. Go ahead and enjoy your gift. I have some business to handle, but we will get up tomorrow," Virgil told him as he watched Derrick open the passenger door.

Derrick walked inside the hotel's doors and straight to the elevator. He pressed the button to the twelfth floor where the penthouses were located. Once he exited the elevator, he found room 1230. He placed his card in the door and heard the door unlock. He opened the door.

He walked cautiously inside until he realized that the room was lit dimly with candles. As he approached the bed he saw a woman lying there wearing just a thong.

He opened his mouth to speak when he felt a soft finger caressing his lips and he was speechless. Derrick was still a virgin and the closest he had gotten to putting his dick in some pussy was when he let one of the hot girls from his school suck his dick.

"My name is Alexis," the woman said. "I am going to fulfill all of your fantasies. Just let me please you, daddy," she said seductively as she pulled his shirt over his head and unbuttoned his jeans.

Derrick's young dick was so hard that he could feel it pulsating in his throat. He was young, but his dick was full grown. Alexis looked at him, then at his dick, and realized that he was a virgin, from the way that he was reacting to what she was doing. She moved her lips to his and kissed him passionately.

Derrick looked at her and his body tensed. He hated feeling as if he was not in control of a situation. Alexis sensed that he was uncomfortable and wanted to diffuse the situation. She grabbed his hands, placed them on her perky titties, and allowed him to explore her body.

His hands felt so soft touching her body that she let her head fall back and allowed the feelings he was creating to spread through her entire body. Derrick squeezed her nipples and then he felt the need to take one of them in his mouth.

His tongue was working magic on Alexis's body as her moans made his dick throb more. Alexis's pussy was creaming and she wanted to feel him inside her. She grabbed him by his hand and pushed him onto the bed.

She untied his Jordans and placed them on the floor. Alexis started to kiss his body from the soles of his feet until she reached his man standing at attention. She studied it for a second and then placed him inside her mouth.

Derrick was mesmerized by the pleasure that he was feeling throughout his body. He lifted his head and watched as Alexis bobbed up and down on his dick. Just as he felt that his body was ready to explode, she removed her mouth and replaced it with her pussy. He let out a moan that sounded as if he was having a heavenly revelation when he felt her walls gripping him. At that moment his mind and body went to another place. He placed his hands on her hips and guided her onto his dick.

Derrick was afraid because this was his first time with a woman, but Alexis showed him what he had been missing. She grinded her hips on him and bounced her ass up and down in slow and methodical motions. His toes began to curl and his moans of pleasures resounded throughout the room.

Alexis could not believe that she was actually breaking someone's cherry. She had just turned eighteen and she was out in the world by herself. When Virgil approached her about making some money, she was down for the cause.

She couldn't even lie, she was about to reach her first orgasm off a virgin that was only sixteen. Alexis gyrated her hips as Derrick continued to pull her further down on his manhood. She felt her body tingling and she knew she was on the verge of explosion.

"Damn, baby, you got this good dick! Oh my God, you 'bout to make me cum!" she said as she sped up the rhythm of her riding.

Derrick also felt his body tensing in a way he'd never felt before, and he knew that this was the feeling that the dudes 'round his way talked about. This was what it felt like to cum inside some pussy. As he felt his first nut coming from the bottom of his feet into the head of his dick, Alexis lowered her body on his and placed her nipple in his mouth.

They both pumped their bodies in a beat that only the two of them could hear. Instantly, in the moment of sex, filled with lust and desire... Derrick and Alexis exploded into a rapturous bliss of euphoria. Alexis then lay her exhausted body on top of Derrick's and allowed him to hold her in his arms.

The two of them did not have any words to say, but the sexual release that they had both experienced spoke volumes. Derrick looked at the woman he was holding in his arms and could see himself with her. He knew that he was going to be connected to this woman in his arms, because she was his first piece of ass. He would think about the two of them later, but what he wanted right then didn't require any talking, just action.

"Alexis, can you do what you did to daddy... that thing that you do with your mouth?" Derrick asked as he let out a laugh.

Alexis raised her head from his chest and looked into his eyes. His bedroom eyes were piercing through to her soul. She could not help but to want to please him in any way that she could. Little did he know that her heart was his, and she didn't even care that he was still in high school.

She smiled at him and said, "Your wish is my command. Just let momma clean you up and I'm really going to show you how to work that big dick of yours!"

Alexis rose from the bed and headed to the bathroom to retrieve a warm washcloth. As promised, she showed him some of the moves that he would use as perfected *techniques with women when he became a full grown man. The two of them fucked and sucked each other until the next morning.*

At checkout time the limo was waiting on the birthday boy as promised. Alexis and Derrick entered the limo, their lives now headed into uncharted territories. Derrick would venture into the game of making money and living life too fast, and Alexis was determined to be by his side, even if that meant being his number two and not his number one.

****

Derrick was snapped out of his thoughts when he heard Alexis speaking to him. He was so lost in his thoughts that he hadn't even heard what she had said.

"My bad, baby, what did you say?" he asked as he took another sip from his glass.

"Damn, daddy, what were you thinking about? The way you were smirking, I could have sworn that you was about to pull out your dick and jack off for me!" Alexis said, laughing at her own comment.

Derrick couldn't help but laugh at her statement. If only she knew that his thoughts did involve his dick and her pussy. "Naw, girl, I was just thinking... you know... going back down memory lane," he said.

"Well I know that this is not the right time or place, but... ahh... stop by the crib sometime this week. You know who wants to see you." With those words said she walked away, leaving him alone.

Alexis didn't know who could be watching them or listening to their conversation, so before someone became suspicious, she left Derrick's side, walking over to mingle with the other guests.

That night Kandice and Derrick made love as if his life depended on it. He was giving the dick so good that Kandice thought she was touching the heavens above. Derrick slid inside his wife and felt his dick throb from the tightness of her walls closing around his shaft. He wanted to bust, but he had trained his dick to control itself.

He slowly grinded inside her, making sure she felt all of his ten inches. Derrick then pulled out, turned her over, and smacked her on her ass. He laid his body on top of hers and plunged back into her pussy. As he fingered her clit, he pumped into her pink hole.

"Oh, shit! Derrrrrick... I'm about to cum!" Kandice shouted.

She felt her body shake. As her juices came down on his dick, leaving her white cream on it, Derrick thrust farther into her and felt his head expand and then explode, sending his soldiers deep inside her womb. He lifted his body from atop his wife and pulled her onto his chest so he could hold her.

That night was filled with so much passion and love, but unfortunately this would be the last time that Kandice would remember getting that kind of sexual satisfaction from her husband. After this night, things between them started to head down a path from which neither of them would be able to return.

ACT 1

CHAPTER 1
Take Care of Home, or The Next Man Will

If you take care of home
You don't have to worry your girl
Take care of home
Take care of home
Maybe if you keep her first
You don't have to worry your girl
Take care of home
Take care of home…
Take Care Of Home… By: Dave Hollister

Two Years Later

Kandice lay on her back and fantasized that any man other than Derrick was fucking her. She went through the typical motions of acting like he was hitting her . Her performance could have won her an academy award for best actress. "Mmm… daddy, hit it harder!" she whispered in his ear.

He began to dig deeper into her walls with his dick, but the motions he was throwing her were some bullshit. It was as if Derrick had stopped giving a fuck about her sexual needs two years ago. She and Derrick had been married for four years and had no children. Although her husband was a good provider, Kandice longed for the days when he hadfucked her until she'd passed out from the pleasure. Now all he did was the same ol', same ol'. Kandice was sexually frustrated! She decided as she lay there pretending to be turned on that starting the next day when her husband left on a business trip, she was going to be a super freak for a man who knew how to give it to her.

Kandice had flirted many times before with the prospect of cheating on her husband, but she'd always hoped for a more satisfying sexual experience with Derrick. She was not into breaking her marriage vows, but with every stoke that he pushed inside her, the more cheating was about to be her reality.

"Damn, girl, this pussy is so good! I'm about to nut all in you!" Derrick said as he released his seed inside her.

Just as soon as he'd started, he was finished. Kandice got up from their king-sized bed and went into the master bathroom. She turned on the hot water in the shower and walked inside her walk-in closet. Quickly locating her Christian Louboutin Maralena Flame sandal shoe box, she retrieved her waterproof Rabbit.

Kandice made sure the door was locked and stepped into the shower. The water was steaming hot and it felt good hitting her skin. She looked at her toy and pushed the on button. The bunny eased onto the tip of her throbbing clit.

"Oh, shit, I don't want to cum yet!" she whispered as sensations of ecstasy raced through her pussy.

She sat down in the tub and spread her legs, getting better access to her pussy. The Rabbit was on full speed. Kandice plunged the head of the vibrator inside her hidden treasure while the bunny ears stimulated her clit. As her right hand handled the Rabbit, her left hand grabbed and pulled on her nipples.

Her mind envisioned the sexy men that she saw daily, and Kandice could no longer control her juices. She pushed the ten-inch vibrator farther inside her. She worked the Rabbit so it would hit the innermost depths of her volcanic cave of orgasmic pleasure. As she pushed the toy farther, faster, and harder into her pussy, she finally busted out all of her pent up sexual frustration.

After her release, she lay on the tub's floor for at least five minutes, letting her orgasm run through her entire body. When she was done enjoying herself, she stayed in the shower an hour longer before washing her body.

While in the shower a smile crossed her lips as she thought about her husband's business trip that he was scheduled to leave for in the morning. For as long as she had been married to Derrick, Kandice had never once been unfaithful. Although she often had many thoughts about fucking other men, she'd never until now had intentions of following through on her urges. She was tired of not being sexually satisfied, and tired of telling Derrick what she needed from him sexually, but still not getting it.

Kandice was no longer going to be Kandice, but another woman who was not going to be disappointed from any more mediocre dick. She was about to become in control of the dick.

CHAPTER 2
Dicked Down

Some say the x, make the sex
Spec-tacular, make me lick you from yo neck
To yo back, then ya, shiverin, tongue deliverin
Chills up that spine, that ass is mine
Skip the wine and the candlelight, no Cristal tonight
If it's alright with you, we fuckin (that's cool)
Deja vu, the blunts sparked, finger fuckin in the park
Pissy off Bacardi Dark
Fuck you Tonight… The Notorious B.I.G

Kandice felt Derrick kiss her on top of her forehead before he left the house for his business trip. She smiled as she thought of what she was planning to do while he was gone—cheat on her husband.

Kontagious

She had been out of the game for over four years, and she had no particular man in mind with whom to share her body, but that was only a small hurdle to overcome. She thought about calling her girlfriend so they could go out on the prowl together, but she quickly changed her mind.

Kandice only had one girlfriend, and Monica had no idea what was going on in her friend's marriage. Although she trusted Monica, Kandice knew better than to tell her business to another female. On this mission of finding dick, Kandice was going to be riding solo.

The silk sheets on the bed were feeling good across Kandice's skin. She could still smell Derrick's cologne lingering in the air. If there was one thing that she could not deny, it was that she still loved her husband. But Kandice felt as if she had her back against a wall when it came to her marriage. She understood that sex was not the be all and end all, but it was important. She had done all that she could think of to make Derrick realize that he was not satisfying her in their bedroom.

She'd even gone as far as suggesting bringing someone else inside their bed. Derrick was appalled when she'd mentioned that. *"What the fuck?" he asked. "How are you going to ask me to share my wife with another man or another woman?"* Was Derrick's response to Kandice's plea for help when it came to their lovemaking.

She closed her eyes and went back to sleep. When she got up for the day, she was going to be ready to take back what she had been holding back for a while now—a good nut.

Across town Chance drove through the city in his black on black Santorini Range Rover while the sounds of Rick Ross filled the vehicle and his dick enjoyed the sucking sensations of wet lips. As slurping sounds mixed with the sounds of Rick Ross's charismatic flow, he could no longer hold back the nut that was coming up and out of his dick and into the woman's warm mouth. Chance grabbed the back of the woman's head and pushed his dick down her throat, making sure that her esophagus accepted every last drop of his cum.

"All right, girl, it's time for you to go," he said once he'd re-zipped his pants and pulled the SUV to the curb. "Here's some money. Now get out my car."

"I know you not going sit here and play me like some common cheap ass ho!" the woman yelled, flabbergasted. "Who the fuck do you think you are, Chance?"

Chance was not normally into dogging women, but he had no problem doing so when he knew they were paper chasing. He wasn't about to get open off of some good head and wife her. He placed his Range Rover in park and flung open the driver's door.

The woman was still sitting in the passenger side wondering what the hell was going on when the door flew open. Chance snatched her out the car by her arm and slammed her back against the hood of the truck. "Bitch, you are not my woman. You're not even my side piece of ass! I suggest you take this fucking money and get the fuck out my sight before I slap the shit out your fucking ass!" he told her as he threw five hundred dollars on the ground.

He then pushed the woman off the hood of his car and closed the door. He swaggered his way to the other side of the truck. Once inside, he cranked up the sounds of Maybach Music and sped off, leaving the woman standing in the street looking stupid.

It was eight forty-five when Chance walked through the doors of Chili's. He grabbed the attention of all of the ladies as he swaggered by in his Diesel Larkee straight-leg jeans, white T-shirt, and all black Jordans. He was looking like the playboy he was as his three-carat pinky ring and earring glistened with each step he took.

"What's up, pimpin'!" Chance said as he approached his crew and ordered a Ciroc and lemonade. J-Rock and Quinton nodded in acknowledgement. Their attention was on the NCAA game showing on the flat screen in front of them.

Chance, J-Rock, and Quinton had been boys since the eighth grade. They became friends when Chance and J-Rock saw Quinton about to get jumped by three other boys from their school. When Chance and J-Rock arrived on the scene, Chance told the main boy that wanted to fight Quinton that he was going to fight Quinton one-on-one, or he was going to fuck him up for being a punk.

After Quinton beat the boy's ass, the three of them jumped the other boys and whipped their asses like they were runaway slaves. From that day on they had become a crew. Now that they were older, they were getting money together, but Chance was the irrefutable leader of the threesome.

While J-Rock and Quinton watched the game, Chance scanned his surroundings. His eyes landed on a woman just entering the restaurant. He was mesmerized by her beauty and style. She wore a pair of boyfriend denim Gucci jeans, a white tank top, orange Python Kelis high heel Gucci pumps, and a Gucci Diamante leather bomber jacket. She carried a Malika orange laminated clutch purse to finish her outfit. He was feeling her style and elegance as she rocked the high end outfit.

But her beauty was what really drew his attention. The woman had the complexion of cappuccino, a smile so bright that a pair of stunnas could not deny its shine, big brown deer eyes, dimples, and lips so succulent that he wanted to suck them until she said stop.

Chance finally heard his name being called, shaking him out of his wandering thoughts.

"Damn, nigga, we talking to your punk ass and you ain't even paying us any attention!" Quinton said as he tapped Chance on his shoulder.

Chance looked at his friend and smiled. "My bad! I was taking in the view. Anyway, let's grab a seat in the corner so we can discuss this business," he said as he walked over to a booth that would put him in the direct line of sight of the woman. "So what's the rundown on what's poppin in the streets?" Chance asked his boys.

As his boys updated him in their coded language, he watched the woman sipping on her drink as she waited for her food to arrive at her table. She appeared to be dining alone.

"What you saying is that everything is everything and everyone is eating?" Chance asked as he turned his attention back to J-Rock and Quinton.

Chance had been in the dope game since he was twenty-five, and his intentions were to retire and go legit by the age of thirty. He had a five-year game plan, and now the loose ends to his master plan were coming together the way he'd hoped. When he got in the game he had no intentions of remaining there. His main objective was to make as much money as he could and then turn his illegal money into legitimate money by washing the dirty money through his diverse business interests. In the last two years Chance had opened two soul food restaurants, a beauty salon, a barber shop, and a bookstore. Now he was looking to get involved in real estate.

J-Rock and Quinton both looked at each other. They had told him everything except the fact that they might have to kill someone who might be a problem to them. Their crew was a close-knit one and they were always leery of newcomers trying to get down with them. This newcomer could potentially be a problem, and they needed to let Chance know.

Quinton finally broke the silence and answered. "You remember 'bout ol' girl who was trying to introduce us to her business partner who's in real estate? Something don't feel right 'bout how she approached us. I can't explain it. I just think we should wait before we proceed with doing business with her, ya dig?"

Chance listened closely to what Quinton was saying. He was right. They needed to be careful when it came to the business of supply and demand. They had been doing well for the past five years and he wanted to keep it that way. He was too close to the finish line to get caught up in the okey doke.

"A'ight, no one make a move on that situation until I give the OK," Chance said as he sipped his drink. "Let's just see if the chick is legit. If she's not, I will be the first one to dome her if need be. That's my word. Set up a meeting."

Chance was young, but he was never one to be stupid. He was cautious and methodical when he executed his business, and he was not into taking unnecessary chances that could get him fed time. That shit was for the birds.

As Chance continued to contemplate his business ventures and going legit, his thoughts were interrupted when he saw the woman that he'd been watching get up to go to the ladies' room. He took this as an opportunity to get at her. He turned to his boys and said that he would be back in a few minutes.

He got up from the booth and walked to the table where she had been sitting. When the waitress passed by, Chance ordered another Ciroc and lemonade for himself and ordered her another glass of whatever she was drinking. The waitress was turning around to leave when the woman sat back down at the table.

The woman did not say anything when she first took her seat. She took in the handsome young man that was sitting across from her. Their drinks were placed in front of them before she said, "When I left to go to the ladies' room, I was dining alone. I come back and here is a strange man before me. To what do I owe the pleasure of your acquaintance?"

Chance was now even more intrigued by this woman. Her words labeled her as classy, and class was always sexy to him. He took another few seconds to take in her beauty. Up close she was even more beautiful than what he had observed when she'd first entered the restaurant. She was the perfect combination of confidence, sexiness, and fineness.

"Let me introduce myself," he finally said. "I'm Chance, and I want you to stay the night with me."

Kandice was captivated by this man's cockiness. His swagger was an instant turn on for. She was looking at a handsome younger man who found her attractive, and she was on a quest for some new dick... the million dollar question was... was she going to be in his bed for the night?

Kandice let out a slight chuckle. "I'm sorry, Chance, I think you have me confused with one of these hood bitches that you usually deal with. That's not how you approach a lady. So let's start this conversation off again. You can call me Kontagious, and what's your name?" she said as she extended her freshly manicured hand for him to shake. Chance smiled, grabbed her hand, and restated his name. "What kind of name is Kontagious?" he asked. "I know that's not the name your momma gave you."

Kandice was getting wet with thoughts of Chance between her legs. She knew from the moment he opened his mouth that she was going to fuck him. It was a plus that the Lance Gross lookalike was fine.

"Hmmm, your name is Chance, is that correct? Well I'm sure you would love to find out why my name is Kontagious. I'll tell you what. I'm feeling your style. Meet me at the Sheraton Hotel downtown, room 920," she told him as she pushed confirm on her iPhone, reserving the room at the hotel. "And make sure that you pay my bill as well," Kandice said as she got up from the table and headed toward her car.

Chance watched the woman he only knew as Kontagious strut out the door. He was thoroughly turned on. He saw visions of him sliding his dick in and out of her all night long. He quickly paid her tab and went back over to the table where J-Rock and Quinton still sat. They were watching him and smiling as he sat back down at the table to join them.

"Yo, Chance, that bitch was bad! I hope you 'bout to hit that, 'cause if not, daddy know just how to give it to her," Quinton said as he smiled at his boy.

Chance looked at his boys and started to laugh. "Naw, dog, I got this. Mommy wants to give it to me, so I'm about to lay down the dick. Thanks anyway for the offer, but I ain't in the business of sharing pussy, ya dig," he said as they all busted out laughing. The three of them kicked it for another thirty minutes before they walked out of the restaurant, going their separate ways. Chance hopped in his Range Rover, cranked up his music, and pulled out of the parking lot. He stopped at the twenty-four-hour Walgreens and bought a box of Trojan Magnum condoms, then headed toward the Sheraton to fuck his mystery woman.

Kandice was waiting for Chance inside the hotel room. After leaving Chili's she had gone home, picked up an overnight bag, and headed to the hotel. She was excited about what she was about to do. After being disappointed with her husband's performance for so long, she anticipated the feel of some new dick.

As she stood in front of the bathroom mirror with nothing on but a thong and a pair of black Dolce & Gabbana pumps, she heard a knock at the door. Although Kandice had just turned thirty-two, she still looked good for her age. She admired her body a few seconds longer, then emerged from the bathroom to open the door.

When she opened the door to let in Chance, she could see the look of shock in his eyes. He wasn't expecting to see such a sight. Kandice stepped aside and let him enter. She then walked to the bar and poured Chance a vodka and pineapple juice, handed it to him, and motioned for him to sit on the bed. Once he was seated, Kontagious, Kandice's alter ego, turned on the stereo that was built into the wall.

Chance watched her with lustful eyes as she performed for him. They had not said one word to each other since he'd entered the room. He had never been with a woman who was about getting to the business of things without the idle chit-chat. He was digging her style and swagger.

As he watched her move her body like a snake to the rhythmic sounds of the old school slow jams blaring through the acoustic speakers, his dick began to swell. She was hypnotizing him with the sexual seduction of her hourglass figure.

Chance watched the show and was enjoying the view when she lowered herself to her knees and unbuttoned his pants, exposing his Emporio Armani boxers. His eyes rolled to the back of his head when he felt her mouth engulf his dick.

Kontagious was giving her all as she gave the stranger head. It had been awhile since she'd given such a good performance. She was enjoying giving him head so much that she started masturbating as her head went up and down on his shaft.

"Damn, girl, you about to make me nut in your mouth! You got some fire head, but I'm trying to feel the inside of your pussy," Chance said as he leaned down and whispered in her ear. His voice was low, but very seductive. For some reason he felt like he needed to make love to this woman rather than fuck her.

He could see her playing with herself and wanted to taste her. He wanted to feel her juices on his tongue. Chance was a freak and he loved to eat pussy, but he didn't eat every woman's pussy. The woman needed to be of a certain caliber to receive that type of treatment from him, and Kontagious was definitely a woman of the right caliber.

Chance placed his hand behind her head and guided her mouth down his nine-inch dick one last time, then he pulled her up from her knees so that her titties were in his face. He grabbed her left breast and placed her nipple in his mouth. She let out a moan and threw back her head as he sucked like a newborn child sucking the breast milk from its mother. Chance guided her thong down her legs without missing a beat.

Once Kontagious was completely naked, Chance told her to lie on the bed. He looked at her body and was amazed at its perfection. Chance took in her smooth, dark skin, slim waist, thick thighs, and phat ass. Not only was her body the complete image of perfection, but so was her face.

Chance dropped his jeans and boxers to the floor. He took two fingers and guided them to her freshly shaven pussy, spreading her lips. His tongue and goatee met her waterfall of crystal clear wetness as he began to devour her with his expert skills of oral pleasure.

Kontagious

Kontagious lay on her back enjoying the sexual assault on her clitoris. She raised her hips, forcing her juices to be consumed by Chance's mouth. She had not experienced this type of pussy eating in quite some time and she was relishing in the moment.

"Uggh... mmm... you are the best, daddy!" Kontagious screamed as she pushed his head farther inside her love. Chance felt her body tighten and release as he tasted her sweet love juices touching his tongue. He reached to the floor and retrieved one of the Magnums from his jeans pocket, then climbed in the bed with Kontagious.

Kontagious looked at him, took the condom from his hands, and placed it in her mouth. She then ventured down onto her hands and knees to the awaiting nine inches of rock hard pipe. With her mouth opened in the shape of an oval, the Magnum slid over his dick, fitting like a glove around his manhood.

Chance watched as she put the protection on and mounted him for the rodeo ride on his stallion. He grabbed Kontagious's hips and pulled her body weight down on him. Her pussy was tight and wet, just the way he liked it.

They began to move their bodies together, and soon the only sound that could be heard was the smacking of balls against ass. The sexual chemistry between them was instantaneous. Kontagious tightened her vaginal muscles around the piece of meat that was hitting her G-spot and continued to wind her hips to the beat of their passion.

Chance grabbed Kontagious by her hair and pulled her head down to his. They locked eyes as their lower regions continued to collide.

"This pussy is so good, girl! Give it to daddy!" he told her as his tongue parted her lips and mingled with hers in a passionate kiss.

Just as passionate as their kiss was, so was the climax they shared simultaneously as Chance exploded in the condom filling the contraceptive with his seed; and Kontagious's pussy juices squirted down the outside of the rubber.

They made love and fucked for the rest of the night as if they had been lovers forever, reuniting after a long separation. They changed in numerous positions, tasted each other, and reached one too many orgasms. By morning they were worn out. And Kandice, aka Kontagious, had finally gotten what she'd wanted and needed—dicked down by some good dick.

CHAPTER 3
Sweetest Love Hangover

I've got the sweetest hangover
I don't wanna get over
Sweetest hangover
Yeah, I don't wanna get over

I don't wanna get
I don't wanna get... over
Ooh, I don't need no cure
I don't need no cure
I don't need no cure

Sweet lovin'
Sweet, sweet, sweet, sweet love
Sweet, sweet love
Sweet, sweet, sweet, sweet love...
Love Hnagover By: Diana Ross

Kandice awakened to find that the man she had shared her body with the previous night holding her tightly against his body as the sun crept through the window. She quietly placed her feet on the plush hotel carpet and proceeded to the bathroom to relieve herself.

As soon as Chance didn't feel Kontagious's body next to his, he opened his eyes to see that she was gone. He looked around the room and was pleased to figure out that she wasn't completely gone, but had only gone to the bathroom. As Chance heard the water in the shower turn on, he debated joining her.

Although Chance wasn't one to be wide open over a woman, there was something about Kontagious that made him want to get to know her and what she was all about. He forced himself out of the king-sized bed and walked to the closed bathroom door.

He knocked on the door before he entered. As he walked into the massive room he could see her washing her body through the clear shower curtain. Chance watched as she lathered the soap in the washcloth and applied the cloth against her skin. She slowly and carefully washed her body. With each touch of the soap against her body, his dick grew harder.

Chance pulled the curtain back and stepped inside the shower. He began to place soft, tender kisses against Kontagious's neck. She leaned her head back as she greedily accepted his kisses. His hands found her erect nipples and began to manipulate them with the tips of his fingers. Chance was young, but he was a skillful lover. He got off from giving pleasure to the woman he was with.

Kandice couldn't take the foreplay any longer. She felt his fingers playing in her garden and it was taking her to the edge of an orgasm. She quickly turned around and kneeled before him. Her mouth found his dick standing at full attention and she feverishly placed all of him inside her mouth.

She sucked and licked until he pulled her off her knees and bent her over in front of him. Chance licked his hand and rubbed it against her pussy, then he eased his nine inches slowly inside her walls and started to give her the business.

As Chance pulled her hips back onto the length of his pole, they found a rhythm that they both could enjoy. Kandice threw it back to him, only intensifying both of their sexual gratification.

"Got damn, I am about to bust this nut! Give me this pussy, girl!" Chance said between gritted teeth.

"Oh, daddy, you can have this pussy anytime you want it! Oh my God, you fucking me so good... I... I... I'm about to cum!" she replied as she picked up the pace of her fingers massaging her clit.

Chance grabbed her hair and felt his sperm coming up to the tip of penis. He quickly pushed her away from his body. Before any of his sperm could hit the shower floor, Kontagious was on her knees to receive every drop of him into her mouth.

The two of them took some time to catch their breath after experiencing yet another dramatic orgasm. After a few minutes of recuperating, they washed each other's bodies before exiting the shower. They decided to order room service and ate breakfast together. Over their meal they talked and got to know each other. Although neither one of them shared too much personal information, they both knew that this was not going to be the last time that they would see each other.

Sex between them was a release for both of them. For Chance it was some good pussy and for Kandice it was a sweet love hangover… compliments of some good dick.

CHAPTER 4
Love/Hate Relationship

Your pushin' buttons, trying to what I'm gonna do
Fussin' and cussin', never put my hands on you
So I'm gonna leave, cause right that just seems best
I'm a grab a few things now and, and I be back for the
rest
I remember good times, but the bad ones don't slip by,
We just been through to much,
And it makes its hard on us when I

I love you so much but I hate you right now,
I love you most times but I hate you some how,
I love you deep down but I hate you come
This love hate relationship is tearing up our house...
Love Hate Relationship By: Dave Hollister

Kandice walked through the door and was immediately greeted by the smell of a Cuban cigar and the sounds of voices. She cursed under her breath because she was not expecting Derrick back until later that night.

She strolled through the foyer, following the voices with her Coach overnight bag in hand and a switch in her hips. When Kandice walked into the family room all eyes fell on her.

"Hey, everyone," Kandice said, greeting her husband and a few of his associates. "How are y'all doing today, fellas?" As Kandice walked closer to Derrick and tried to kiss him, he looked at his wife, and his relaxed demeanor turned tense as he took in the outfit that she was wearing.

"Where the hell you coming from with that little ass skirt on, showing all of my goods for the world to see!?" Derrick asked loudly as he grabbed her arm. The room got quiet as Derrick's associates watched the domestic dispute unfold.

Kandice yanked her arm from his grasp, looked him in his eyes, and said, "Is this the first thing that you say to your wife after being away?" She stared at him as if she was challenging him in before she turned and walked away.

As Kandice's stilettos clicked across the Rosa Aurora marble tile, the sound of a pair of Timberland boots walking behind her gained momentum. Derrick grabbed her arm again, making her turn to face him.

"Who the fuck you think you talking to? I asked you a fucking question, and you better give me a response!" Derrick yelled as he pulled her by her arm up the stairs leading into their master bedroom.

Kandice remained quiet as she was being pulled upstairs. When she initially came home she was feeling remorse for cheating, but now with the way Derrick was showing his ass, her guilty feelings quickly changed to ones of satisfaction.

Derrick pushed his wife inside their bedroom and quickly shut and locked the door. "What the fuck is this?" he asked, noticing for the first time the overnight bag she carried. "You fucking another nigga and coming back from your night's escapade?" He grabbed the bag from her hand and unzipped it to see what was inside.

Pulling out the clothes from the bag, he threw each piece of clothing onto the bed. Kandice watched the spectacle that was taking place in front of her and she smirked as she reminisced on the fucking she took the night before.

Derrick turned and saw the smirk across his wife's face and became enraged. "What the fuck you laughing at me? Huh? What the fuck is so fucking funny, Kandice?" he shouted as he stepped closer to her.

Kandice remained calm. She looked into his eyes and responded. "Baby, why are you tripping? I went out last night with Monica. I got fucked up and I stayed the night at her house. I left this bag of clothes over there from the last time I ended up spending the night there. I'm your wife. Why would I ever cheat on you when you take such good care of me?"

Derrick wanted to smack the shit out of her for lying to him. He knew she was out doing something that she had no business doing. There was no direct evidence of her doing wrong, though, and he was wrong for even sweating her on that front, because he was doing something far worse than what he thought she was doing. He was living a lie, and had been for a long time.

Kandice started taking off her clothes and heading toward the bathroom. She was down to her lace bra and underwear when she felt Derrick's eyes roaming her body. A feeling of passion swept over her.

This was the first time in a while that he had looked at her as if he wanted her. Derrick looked at his wife's curves and wanted to push his dick inside her. He took two steps forward and stood in front of her. His hand caressed her face as he took in her beauty.

Kandice closed her eyes and enjoyed his touch. She had been waiting for him to show her some type of intimacy for a long time, and she wanted to savor this moment. But then the hand that had been caressing her face was now wrapped around her throat and started to squeeze. Kandice opened her eyes as her breaths became shallow.

"Derrick, what are you doing? You're hurting me," she whispered with the little bit of breath she could still muster.

Derrick tightened his grip around her neck and said, "You are my wife! You better not be giving my pussy away, 'cause if I find out that you letting the next nigga hit my pussy, I'm going to kill you!"

He let go of her neck and allowed her to regain her breath. Before he left the room Derrick grabbed Kandice's face and kissed her lips. He looked at her as she watched him with eyes that were filled with terror. Derrick hated putting his hands on his wife, but he had to keep her in check. He needed to make sure that she knew he was not going to stand for her fucking around on him. Although Derrick had no evidence that she had cheated, he had to deter her from even thinking about committing the act.

"Now go clean yourself up and put on something decent," he said.

Kandice wiped the tears from her eyes, walked into the bathroom, and locked the door behind her. She waited until she heard the bedroom door close before she broke down crying. This was the first time in a long time that Derrick had laid his hands on her.

Kandice was conflicted with so many emotions. Derrick had been such a good man to her until his mother had died two years prior. They'd had their fights, but it had not gotten physical between them in quite some time.

After the night she had spent with Chance she was re-evaluating whether she was even willing to continue to put up with the bullshit. "I'm too good of a fucking woman to be having this nigga put his hands on me," Kandice said to herself.

She turned on the water in the shower when the sounds of L.T.D.'s "Stranger" blared through the speaker of her iPhone. Kandice smiled because she had given that ringtone to Chance. Jeffery Osborne's voice shouted, "Ooh la la la la la la la la la la la la la Nobody, na na na na Ooh la la la la la la la la la la la la la Nobody, na na na na Ooh la la la la la la la la la la la la la Nobody, na na na na Was nobody to care after me."

Kandice listened to the ringtone and waited for the call to go to her voicemail. Then she stepped into the shower and washed her body. The cascading water concealed her tears as her mind wandered to happier times in her life and in her marriage.

After allowing herself to relax in the shower, Kandice exited, feeling better. Soaking wet with her towel wrapped around her body, she walked back into the bedroom. She was shocked when she saw Derrick sitting on the bed waiting for her.

There was silence between them as both of them waited for the other to speak first. Derrick finally broke the silence and said, "Come here and sit on the bed next to me." He winked and patted the spot next to him, signaling for her to sit down.

Kandice slowly moved in his direction. She wanted to tread carefully, because she had no idea what kind of mood he was in, and she did not want another physical altercation. With the towel still attached to her body, Kandice placed her body next to her husband.

Derrick locked eyes with his wife and leaned his head in her direction. He licked her lips with his tongue and tasted her. Kandice jerked her head away from his kiss.

"Kandice, look, I'm sorry, ma, for the way that I came at you earlier. I had no right to put my hands on you, and that was a bitch move that I did. I'm sorry.

Please forgive me. You are my wife and we are in this for better or worse," Derrick said as he tried to be sincere.

Kandice heard what he was saying, but she was still upset about the situation. She wanted her marriage to work, but if something did not change between them, starting with their sex life, Kandice didn't see them making it.

"Derrick, it's not just about what happened between us today. We have been having problems for a minute now. I don't know what has been going on with you, but for the last two years things have been fucked up between us. Is there something that I've done to make you not want me anymore?" Kandice asked with tears of sadness falling from her eyes.

Derrick knew that he had been giving Kandice his ass to kiss lately. Ever since his mother had passed, he wasn't the same person. He was emotionally torn and took his frustrations out on Kandice. In that moment Derrick understood that he was losing his wife, and he needed to keep her satisfied in order for him to save his marriage.

"Look, you're right. There are some things that I have been going through that I can't share with you that have had me stressing. We are going to be all right. Let me show you how much I need you."

Kontagious

Derrick pulled the towel away from his wife's body. He knew he had to dick her down good to ensure that she was happy. His dick was rock hard and he wanted to feel her tight, creamy insides. Derrick glided his hand across her nipple and felt its firmness. He licked his lips and placed them on her chocolate breast.

Derrick's tongue sent sensations of ecstasy throughout Kandice's body. She placed her hand on the back of his head and pushed his mouth farther onto her nipple. As he sucked on her nipple she felt his hand parting her pussy lips, and his index finger began to massage her clit.

"This feels so good, baby. Please make love to me." Kandice said in a voice begging for something that she had been longing for from her husband. She needed to feel wanted.

Derrick pushed her wet body onto the bed. He looked at her from head to toe as his finger plunged inside her and the juices began to pop from within her pussy. The sounds from her heated oven echoed within the bedroom's walls.

His dick was rock hard and he wanted to enter her pussy to relieve his throbbing, but he had to remind himself that she needed to get hers before he got his.

Konatgious

Derrick dropped to his knees, stuck his tongue inside her, and began making love to her pussy.

He wrapped her legs around his neck and plunged his tongue into her warm cave of femininity. Derrick could hear the moans escaping Kandice's mouth. Her whimpers of pleasure resonated in his ears and made his dick even harder.

"Derrick!!" was the only word that Kandice could say as she released her love into her husband's mouth.

Derrick undressed himself and admired Kandice's body. As he looked at her he could not deny that he had much love for her and he wished that things could be different. He climbed into the bed with his wife, pushed the head of his dick inside her, and felt his dick expand even more.

Kandice couldn't take it anymore. She needed all of him inside her. She propelled her body toward his manhood, making her pussy accept his dick whole. She shivered as a sensation of sexual bliss spread throughout her body.

Kandice had been praying for this to happen. She had been waiting for her husband to fuck her like he wanted her again. The two of them made love for the rest of the afternoon

Nikki Urban

In that one night Kandice forgot about all the reasons why she'd begun to hate her husband and concentrated on the love that she felt in his arms. And even if it were for one day only, she was going to make the best of what she now had.

ACT II

CHAPTER 5
Shit Don't Add Up

Money money money money, money (x6)
Some people got to have it
Some people really need it

Listen to me y'all, do things, do things, do bad things
with it
You wanna do things, do things, do things, good things
with it
Talk about cash money, money

Talk about cash money- dollar bills, yall
For the love of money
People will steal from their mother
For the love of money
People will rob their own brother
For the love of money
People can't even walk the street
Because they never know who in the world they're gonna
beat

Kontagious

For that lean, mean, mean green
Almighty dollar, money…
For the Love of Money… by: The O'Jays

Kandice sat in her office at her boutique, A Diva's Swagg where the store sold high end women clothes, shoes and accessories, as she went over some business paperwork when she realized that she needed to make a bank deposit. She glanced at her watch and saw that it was four pm.

"Shit, I need to make this run to the bank before they close at five," she said out loud as she turned in her chair to face the windows behind her. She bent over and punched in the code to the hidden safe that was built inside the floor under the floor rug.

When she opened the safe she saw that almost twenty thousand dollars needed to be deposited. Kandice leaned back in her executive leather chair and began filling out four different deposit slips. She knew that any deposits that totaled over ten thousand dollars could trigger the bank to file a Suspicious Activity Report and an IRS audit into her business affairs. One thing that Kandice despised was people in her business.

When she opened her business Kandice made sure to have multiple bank accounts for times like this when she had lump sums of money that needed to be deposited. After a few days of the money being in the accounts she would transfer the funds into the single account from which she paid payroll and handled her business expenses.

Kandice grabbed the money, the bank slips, her car keys, her purse, and headed out the door. As she drove her black on black CL550 coupe Benz, the Sirius XM R&B station played Atlantic Star's "Secret Lovers." Kandice turned up the stereo, causing the song to blare louder through the acoustic speakers in the car.

She started singing the lyrics to the song as her mind wandered back to the night she'd spent with Chance. Although things were going all right now between her and Derrick, Kandice wanted to see Chance again. She wondered if he'd thought about her since that night, and if he wanted to see her as well.

Kandice arrived at the first bank, parked her car, and went in to make her deposit. She did this three more times at various banks and then went back to the store to close it down for the night. She had given her only sales associate, Marshane, the day off, and Kandice was shutting down shop early.

Inside her purse were the deposit receipts with each account balance. Kandice pulled out the slips of paper and began to read the balances. Immediately she knew something was wrong because the balances were off. She was always meticulous when it came to her paperwork and managing what went in and out of her accounts, and she knew the balances were not right.

She turned on her laptop and checked each bank through the online banking system. What she realized was that she was missing about fifty thousand dollars. Kandice was dumbfounded. She knew that she wasn't stealing from herself, and Derrick didn't have access to her accounts because she'd made sure to put of all her bank accounts in her maiden name only.

"What the fuck!" was all that she could think to say.

Then a thought came to her. What if Marshane had something to do with the missing money? The only question was, if that was the case, how was she doing it, because Kandice was the only one who made the bank deposits, and the drawer never once came up short while Marshane worked at the boutique.

All Kandice knew was that the money didn't add up to what she knew she was supposed to have in the bank. And she was about to get to the bottom of what was going on as soon as possible. Kandice Googled the local spy shop and looked at their Web site. When she saw what she was looking for, she wrote down the address and headed out the door.

CHAPTER 6
Reminisce

I stumbled on this photograph
It kinda made me laugh
It took me way back
Back down memory lane

I see the happiness... I see the pain
Where am I... back down memory lane

I see us standing there
Such a happy happy pair
Love beyond compare
Look-a-there look-a-there…
Memory Lane By: Minnie Riperton

Chance was headed to a meeting that J-Rock had set up. As he drove, his mind wandered back to his childhood. He'd grown up privileged because his father was the neighborhood dope man. Although he was young and his parents tried to shield him from what his father's true job was, he was far from a dummy. He'd known exactly what business his pops was in. A few days before his twenty-fifth birthday, he had a talk with his mother, who had schooled him to a few simple rules to live by if he was going to play the game. As he rode in silence, he remembered the words his mother spoke to him that day. Chance was dibbling and dabbling in some small time hustling. He was seeing small change and was trying the ropes. He purposely waited until he was out of high school and out of his parents' house before he thought about getting money on the streets.

Chance was in his room putting some money in his top dresser drawer when his mother walked in. He was so engrossed in what he was doing that he had not even heard her enter his apartment with the key she had.

She stood in the doorway of his bedroom and watched as her son put up his money. As she stood there watching him, her thoughts screamed, "This nigga need to be more on point with his surroundings. I could have been a nigga trying to rob and kill him."

Chance felt eyes beating into the back of his head and his instincts told him to turn around. When he did he saw his mother watching him.

"Boy, if you going to be in the streets, you need to be on point at all times. You never know when someone is plotting for your downfall," were the first words out of his mother's mouth.

Chance nodded since he could do nothing but agree with what she was saying. She was absolutely right. He had been caught slippin'. Thankfully, the person who was there was not there to bring him harm, but he might not be so lucky next time.

"You right, Ma. But what you know about what I'm doing? Why is it whenever a young nigga got a little bit of change he got to be getting it from the streets?" he asked, already knowing that this was not the case for him. His money was dirty, just as dirty as his father's money. "Boy, please! I still keep my ear to the streets. The streets do talk. All you have to do is listen and you will hear all that you need to know. Don't think for one moment that because I work a respectable job, I have no idea what be going on." She smiled and took a seat on his bed, motioning for him to sit next to her. Once Chance sat next to his mother, she continued.

"Look, Chance, I am not here to judge you or try to run your life. Your father and I tried to shield you from this. This is not the life that either one of us wanted for you, but you are a grown man, and you will make your own decisions.

"But let me run a few rules down for you. First off, never leave product where you lay your head. Second, never use the product that you're selling. Third, never talk business on the phone. Always meet in person to handle that. Fourth, never let people know your inner thoughts, because if they know your weaknesses, they will move on you. Fifth, a flashy nigga is always a nigga that will get caught. Sixth, remember, this game is not played in checkers, but in chess. Make sure each move you make is played strategically. Last, being greedy will be your downfall if you are not careful. Make your money and leave the game." His mother had just given her lil'man some jewels of wisdom. She hoped that he would heed her words and apply them when necessary.

Chance smiled now as he thought about that conversation. That was almost five years ago, and now here he was at the end of his game plan that had started the night his mother had bestowed that advice on him. After that discussion, he'd known that he needed to talk with his pops man to man.

His pops was skeptical of Chance's plan, but Chance wasn't asking for any handouts, so there wasn't much his pops could say. He didn't want to make his money based off the strength of who his pops was. He wanted to make his own way, and that was exactly what he'd done.

As he turned a corner on his way to his meeting, Chance saw a woman who looked just like Kontagious. His dick got instantly hard as he thought about his rendezvous with her. He had to know if this woman was Kontagious, so he busted a quick U-turn in the middle of the street and parked his truck directly behind the Benz that this woman had entered, blocking its path of exit. When the driver opened the door and stepped out to tell him to move, he saw the exact woman for whom he was looking. He jumped out of his truck and walked up to her. They were both silent as they looked at the other. Chance stepped closer to her, putting little to no space between them as he leaned in and placed his juicy lips on hers.

She kissed him back as if they were making up from a fight. He sucked her lip and placed his tongue inside her mouth. Their tongues danced to a beat all their own as the kiss continued for what seemed to be an eternity.

Kandice pushed Chance back from her so she could catch her breath and stop the juices in her panties from dripping. "You can't be stalking me," she said. "Then you have the nerve to kiss me like you're my husband." She chastised him, but deep down she was happy to see him again.

Chance looked at her and she was still as perfect to him as he remembered. "Kontagious, all that shit you talking, I'm not tryin' to hear. All I want to know is when am I going to see you again?"

Kandice, aka Kontagious, could do nothing but smile, because his arrogant and cocky confidence turned her on. The fucked up thing was that she was contemplating seeing him again, although she and her husband were trying to work out their marriage.

Kontagious

Chance looked at his watch and realized that he was running late. He looked at the woman he knew as Kontagious and said, "I have to go. I'm running late for a meeting. But I meant what I said. I'm trying to see you, ma, and soon," he told her as he kissed her again.

This time as they engaged in their kiss Chance made sure to leave her with something to think about. He unzipped her pants and slid his hand inside her lace underwear. His finger flickered back and forward on her clit as his thumb slid inside her pink opening.

Kandice moaned softly as he molested her. At that moment she didn't give a fuck that she was outside and that people could be watching her. She spread her legs farther apart and allowed him to plunge his thumb deeper inside her. Kandice moved her hips forward as she rocked to the pace of his thumb going in and out of her.

Kandice placed her arm around Chance's neck and moaned in his ear as the bottom half of her body sped up the pace to his finger fucking. "Oh, shit, feel my pussy cum," she whispered seductively in his ear as her body shook and she released on his thumb.

Chance removed his hand from her pants, zipped them back up, and licked his thumb. He leaned in once more and kissed. "Text me. We need to finish this," he said as he jumped back in his Range and drove off, heading toward his meeting.

CHAPTER 7
Meeting of the Minds

Play it cool, that's the old school rule, man
Keep your ears to the street, y'all never lose man
Make your enemies believe there's love there
Cause in war, belief is all fair
Rock them to sleep, shots in your jeep
And you ain't never know the plot was from me
It's from my Masterminds

A Mastermind - Sees it coming before it comes
A Mastermind - Before he go to war he counts his one
A Mastermind - Everything planned out perfect, in case
y'all niggaz got to get murdered
A Mastermind - Sleeps at night, real easy
A Mastermind - Cause everything he does is by the book
A Mastermind - Never do a thing irrational, lives forever,
these tales are classical…
Mastermind By: Nas

Kontagious

The woman walked inside the restaurant and was escorted by the hostess to a secluded spot where only people who had the right money could venture. She strutted to the table wearing a black matte one-sleeved Michael Kors jersey dress, gold Christian Louboutin Maggie glitter and snakeskin platform pumps, gold bracelets on her wrist, and carrying a Gucci GG Plus briefcase. As she walked closer to her awaiting party, she could feel the lustful eyes of her potential clients roaming her one-hundred-thirty-pound body, wishing that they could feel the insides of her pussy.She finally reached the table and stood in front of it as she extended her hand. "Good evening, gentlemen. It is my pleasure to make your acquaintance," she said. They all shook hands and greeted each other.

The private waiter approached the table and the four people ordered their alcoholic beverage of choice. When the waiter scattered off to place their drink orders, the business meeting commenced. J-Rock introduced Chance and Quinton to the woman.

J-Rock had met the woman that sat across from them when he'd sat next to her on a first-class flight from Georgia. She explained that she was a partner in Empire Real Estate Brokerage Firm, LLC, where they only dealt in high-end properties.

Once J-Rock knew what she did, he made sure to get her business card. But what he never told Chance and

Quinton was that something did not sit well with him about this woman after he ran into her again a few times after their flight. In his line of work, bumping into someone on various occasions was not usually a coincidence, but because he knew Chance was trying to get into the real estate game, he figured she could be their connection in if everything checked out.

The waiter returned with their drinks just as the woman placed her Gucci briefcase on the table, opened it, and pulled out a leather portfolio.

"Chance, J-Rock informed me that you are interested in getting into real estate. This is our business portfolio. It shows our assets, our properties, a list of some of our clients, before and after pictures of some of our properties, projected revenue for the upcoming year, and a synopsis of our past and future business endeavors," the woman stated as she slid a company folder with the information in it over toward Chance for his review.

As Chance looked over the portfolio, the woman sipped her amaretto sour. She was reading his facial expressions as he looked at the provided data in front of him. She hoped that Chance saw the potential in investing his money with the company.

"Excuse me, gentlemen. I'm going to excuse myself to the ladies' room as you look over the portfolio. If you have any questions, I will be more than happy to answer them when I return," she said as she left the table and headed to the restaurant's facilities.

The woman entered the bathroom and checked to make sure that no one else was in there with her. When she was reassured that the room was empty, she locked the door for privacy. She pulled out her BlackBerry and began to send out a text. The woman then relieved herself and washed her hands. Her phone vibrated, alerting her that she'd received a text response.

She read the text and quickly typed in her response. The phone vibrated once again and she read the message before unlocking the door to return to the table. As she approached the table she saw the three men talking.

"I hope that I was not gone too long and that you found the information provided to you useful in making your decision, Chance?" she asked as she took her seat. Chance rubbed his hands together as he thought about all that he had read. What he saw excited him, but he needed to think about the opportunity before he jumped in feet first.

"Let me ask you something," Chance said. "So you say that you're a partner at Empire. So why is it that you're here alone and not with your partner?"

The woman smiled. She could tell that the man before her was no fucking dummy and he wanted to know exactly who he is dealing with. "Chance, it's true that I am a partner. However, part of my job function is to meet with potential clients, get an idea of what their needs are as far as real estate, and answer their preliminary inquiries. Then once the client has decided to do business with Empire, a meeting will be set up between the client and Mr. Arnold, the other partner."

Chance and the woman studied each other. They were sizing up each other in some sort of power struggle. Then it occurred to him… they were having a meeting of the minds.

Chance raised his glass and saluted her, liking what he saw. The four of them then sat and discussed the potential of Chance investing in some of Empire's properties and what his return would look like. The group laughed and talked business until Chance felt convinced that this was a good hustle that would make him the money he needed to get out of the game for good.

CHAPTER 8
It Is What It Is

I though it was love
Didn't wanna admit that
When I looked back
It was lust
Too bad I had to learn a lesson
The're against me
You were with me
But you never let your old thang go
I don't care to know why
Girl I guess some things
Can't be explained
It is what it is (what it is)
I don't know what to call it
'Cause I'm feelin' something else (I'm feeling something else)

It is what it is (what it is)
Just don't let yourself get caught up (uh huh)
When it's really something else…

It Is What It Is By: Usher

As Chance was concluding his business, he got a call from Kontagious. Chance jumped in his Range Rover and pulled off, heading for his destination. He was looking forward to seeing her again and feeling her wet pussy wrapped around his dick. Just the thought of being inside her made his dick hard with excitement.

Chance pulled up to the Kontagious's Boutique at the same time as her. He watched her walk to the door and fumble in her purse, looking for the keys to unlock the door. Chance exited his car and walked up behind her. When he was directly behind her he placed his arm around her waist and pulled her into his body.

Kandice had seen him when he'd pulled up to the store, so she was not alarmed when he walked up behind her. She allowed his touch to soothe her body.

"I was wondering when you were going to get out of the car," Kandice said as she pushed the store's door open.

"Hmmm, I see that you are observant, ma. I like that... a woman who pays attention to her surroundings at all times," Chance stated as he turned her around so she was facing him.

The two of them stared at each other for a few seconds. The sexual chemistry between them was fucking crazy, and they knew it, but Kandice wanted to clear the air with him so that he understood the rules to the game before they went any further.

"Chance, before—" She didn't get the opportunity to complete her sentence because Chance had parted her mouth with his tongue. Their tongues danced in a rhythm that was synonymous with their passion. Kandice needed to speak, but her pussy was calling for his dick. She slightly pushed him slightly away and looked at him. "Look, I already know what you want to tell me," Chance said before she could speak. "I understand that you got a man. I understand that you stepping out on your dude. But when you with me, you are with me, so fuck him. Even if this shit between us is on some creep shit for right now, I'm cool with that. But just let it be known, you will be my woman before the shit is all said and done. It is what it is for now."

Kandice was speechless. It was as if he could read her mind and he understood what her situation was. She was feeling him even more now, and his cockiness was making her pussy cream for him to be inside her.

She laughed and responded. "I see this is not your first rodeo. I respect your gangsta and I respect you for understanding my situation. Before we go any further, let me tell you my real name. It's Kandice."

Chance smiled, glad that she had felt comfortable to give him her government, but he didn't mind calling her by her alias. He actually thought that it was a cute pet name, because she was contagious, and he wanted what she had.

"That's your government name, but to me you will always be Kontagious," he said. Chance lifted her body, placed her on the counter, and proceeded to kiss her again.

His kisses were soft and tender and Kandice greedily accepted every one of them. Chance's hands smoothly roamed her body as he ventured down and assaulted the sacred treasure between her legs.

Kandice moaned as Chance captivated the essence of her body. She spread her legs farther apart as she felt his finger slide in and out of her. "Damn, daddy, you feel so good. I need you inside me," she told him as she nibbled on his ear.

Chance wasn't in any rush. He wanted to enjoy bringing her pleasure, and he was not ready to invade her. He undressed her slowly, making sure to lust after each part of her body. In his eyes Kandice was perfect, and he wanted to take in all of her beauty.

"You are beautiful, Kontagious," Chance said as he admired her figure.

Kandice was flattered. It had been so long since her husband had given her any positive feedback. She felt needed and wanted as Chance spoke the words that her ears had longed to hear.

Chance dropped to his knees so he was eye level with Kandice's pussy. He rubbed his hand over the lips, causing her body to shiver. With his fingers gently playing with her clit, he used his tongue to spread her lips.

Kandice was in heaven as she felt Chance stabbing her pussy with his tongue. His head game was like none she had ever experienced before. She grabbed the top of his head, placing her hands on the waves in his head, and guided his head farther inside her.

"Oh my God! Please, stop! I can't take it anymore!" she pleaded, hoping that he would bring her to an orgasm with his dick.

Chance stepped back and undressed himself, leaving on only his Calvin Klein boxers. He pulled his dick out through the slit and stroked his oversized package to its full capacity. Then he stepped closer to Kandice and entered her slowly.

They both let out a simultaneous moan of desire. They began to move their bodies as if they were dancing to an African drum beat. Neither of them were in a rush to cum, so they kept a steady and slow pace.

Chance grabbed Kandice's ass and pulled her body deeper onto his dick. The sensation of her pussy juices engulfing his dick made the head of his dick pulsate, causing him to expand wider inside her cave.

Chance was in a sexual haze of ecstasy as the words of the Isley Brothers song left his lips. "You're contagious, touch me baby, give me what you got, sexy lady, drive me crazy, drive me wild." He dug deeper into her pussy and Kandice pushed back harder and faster.

Chance placed his hand around Kandice's neck and applied pressure. Her pussy got wetter as the feeling of losing her breath mixed with the intoxication of her pussy getting ready to explode. She placed her finger on her clit and moved it in a circular motion.

Suddenly their bodies exploded together from the inside out. They both experienced orgasms so strong that they were left completely drained. Chance loosened his hands from around Kandice's neck and kissed her lips.

"I'm sorry that I choked you," he said as he looked at her.

Chance was freaky in every sense of the word. He was not trying to kill her when he choked her. He just enjoyed the act of choking during sex, especially if the pussy was good. He hoped that his freakiness did not scare Kandice, because his intentions were never to bring Kandice pain, but only pleasure.

Although that was the first time Kandice had experienced erotic asphyxiation, surprisingly she had enjoyed it. Chance had just turned her on to a new way of having an orgasm that was like nothing she had felt before.

"Baby, don't worry about that," she said as she kissed the man that was about to be her boo on the side. "You just made me have one of the best nuts that I have had in my lifetime."

They stayed in the store for some time longer talking and ironing out the details for their relationship. Kandice even felt comfortable enough to tell Chance that her husband's mother had passed two years ago, and ever since then her husband had not been the same, which had made her seek out a relationship with another man.

Chance felt a sense of peace while in Kandice's presence. This woman was built for a nigga like him. He could tell that she was lacking in confidence, although she tried to perpetrate through her hard exterior. He could sense that the nigga who had made her his wife was not treating her like the queen that she was, and that had damaged her spirit. Chance was going to change that, but right now he had to play his position.

The situation was what it was. Chance's plan was to wait in the shadows for the opportunity to make Kandice his woman. He felt in his soul that she was meant for him. The wrong man had gotten to her before he had the chance to crown his queen, but he planned on fixing that mistake as soon as possible.

ACT III

CHAPTER 9
Business as Usual

But it's business as usual
Day after day
Business as usual
Just grinding away
You try to be righteous
You try to do good
But business as usual Turns your heart into wood...

Business as Usual By: The Eagles

"Alexis, where you at?" Derrick shouted as he walked into the apartment that he kept on the other side of town. He sat down on the white Italian leather sofa and turned on the TV.

A few minutes later she appeared from another room. She stepped into the living room wearing a Coogi sweater dress and some flip flops.

"What the fuck took you so long?" he asked. "You better not have another man in here around my son!" Derrick said as he eyed the curves on his baby's mother.

"Nigga, please! The only thing that you and I have to discuss is business! Furthermore, who I let between my legs is none of your concern!" Alexis said as she sat in the chair in front of Derrick. Alexis had been with Derrick since he was sixteen. Two years prior to his mother's death and his marriage to his wife, Alexis became pregnant, and they were now parents to a son whom she'd name after her child's father—Derrick Jr.

Alexis had gotten upgraded from baby momma to business partner four years ago when Chance had married Kandice. He had hired her to be a partner in his business and given her this apartment. When Alexis found out that he was going to marry someone else, she was devastated. She always thought that she was going to be the one to have his last name, especially since she had given Derrick a child. In any relationship there were going to be ups and downs, and from her perspective, this was Derrick's and hers down time. She was more than confident that they would be together again.

"What happened with the meeting?" he asked as he pushed the off button on the remote so that he could give her his undivided attention.

Alexis was indeed a hood chick who was down to make her own dough, but most importantly she was down for Derrick 100 percent. Although she and Derrick were not an item at the present time, Alexis was always present in Derrick's life. She was Derrick's best friend, and he was hers. A few years back when Derrick approached Alexis with a proposition to make some dough, she was all with it. "They were a little skeptical about it at first, but I was able to make their doubts seem trivial," she answered. "From the way the conversation went, it sounds as if the chief in charge needs convincing."

Derrick listened to her and let her words marinate in his brain. His entire empire depended on people like the people Alexis met with. Since he had tapped into a hustle that was making him money on top of money, he had to keep the money flowing, and people like this potential client were imperative to making that happen.

"When are you meeting them again?" Derrick asked as he walked to the window and peered outside.

"They didn't say. The only thing they told me was that they would get back at me when they had an answer."

Kontagious

Alexis walked over to Derrick and looked into his eyes. He stared deep into her eyes, giving Alexis the feeling that he was trying to decipher her innermost thoughts. She didn't like that.

She broke the gaze by dropping to her knees and unbuckling his Armani Collezioni silk linen pants. Once the zipper was undone, Alexis reached into the split of his boxers and pulled out his manhood. She had placed her mouth on his dick when his cell phone rang, disrupting the mood.

Derrick stepped back from the warmth of Alexis's mouth and took the call. He listened without saying a word. The call ended and he resumed his position, allowing Alexis to put his dick back in her mouth.

After he busted off in her mouth, he was going to wet his dick in her pussy and check on his son before riding out to handle his business. The call that he'd just received was one that he had been anticipating.

Later as his hot lava of cum shot through his body and ended inside the condom, he looked at Alexis and really saw her for the first time in a long while. Although she was the mother of his only child, he'd married Kandice because she had stolen his heart. What he shared with Alexis was love mixed with business. He could not deny that he loved Alexis, but he was not about to leave his wife to be with her. For now all that he could give her was their business arrangement, but maybe one day in the future they could rekindle what they once had before shit got complicated between them.

CHAPTER 10
Cleaning Out the Closet

Skeletons in your closet
Itchin' to come outside
Messin' with your conscience
In a way your face can't hide

Oh things are gettin' real funky
Down at the old corral
And it's not the skunks that are stinkin'
It's the stinkin' lies you tell

What did your mama tell you about lies
She said it wasn't polite to tell a white one
What did your daddy tell you about lies
He said one white lie turns into a black one

So, it's gettin' ready to blow
It's gettin' ready to show

Nikki Urban

Somebody shot off at the mouth and
We're getting ready to know...
Skeletons By: Stevie Wonder

Kandice walked into Virgie's house for the first time since Derrick's mother had passed four years ago. She was there to clean the house and get it ready for the movers to put Virgie's possessions in a storage unit. Derrick wanted to go to Virgie's house and clean it himself, but he could not bring himself to go through with it, especially since he had finally decided to place the house on the market for sale.

As she walked inside the house where her husband had grown up, she looked around and realized that her mother-in-law was a borderline hoarder.

"Let me find out that Virgie was a hoarder! Damn, look at all this shit in the house! Where the hell am I going to start first?" Kandice said out loud as her eyes roamed the clutter in the living room.

She decided to start in the back of the house and work her way to the front. She walked to the back where the bedrooms were located and entered Virgie's bedroom. Placing her purse on the bed, she sighed.

Kandice looked around the room and decided that she would start in the closet first. Surprisingly, the inside of the closet was quite organized. She stepped inside the closet and proceeded to remove the clothes from the hanging bar. As Kandice grabbed a handful of clothes, her foot got caught in a crack in the hardwood flooring. Her heel got stuck deep within the crevice of the opening and she had to bend down and remove her shoe in order to step back out of the closet.

When she bent down to retrieve her shoe, Kandice noticed that the opening in the floor had something hidden underneath. Being nosey, she wanted to see what was concealed below, so she got down on all fours and removed the single board of hardwood flooring, and that was when she realized that there was more than one hardwood board loose.

"What the fuck! What the hell did Virgie have going on in here?" Kandice wondered aloud as she lifted five boards.

Her eyes got wide when she saw that there were piles of rubber-banded money stacked under the floor. Kandice pulled the money from its location and placed the piles on the bed. After she'd removed all the money, she went back over to the hiding place in the closet to see if she'd missed anything.

Underneath the money there were documents, pictures, and papers. She pulled out the items one by one, being careful not to tear any of the papers. But before she could look at the papers, she heard someone walk into the house.

She quickly rushed to the bed and pushed all of the money and the papers inside her oversized Coach tote, grabbed the purse from the bed, placed it snugly on her arm, and took out her .22 that she kept in the purse's inside pocket. Kandice quietly stepped inside the closet, pulled the door closed until it was only cracked, and waited to see who was coming for her. She was shocked when she heard her name being called from the other room. Kandice did not move for fear of walking into a trap. She listened closely as the sounds of steps got closer and then came to a stop in the bedroom.

"Kandice, it's Virgil. I know you're in here. I just spoke with Derrick and he told me you were here."

Kandice grabbed her steel tighter, making sure that her finger was securely on the trigger. She kicked the closet door open with her little bitch pointed at Virgil. When the door flung open it startled Virgil. When he saw the .22 pointed at him, a smile crossed his lips.

"Virgil, you and my husband are friends, but you and I are not. Why the fuck are you stalking me?" Kandice asked as she circled around him, edging herself closer to the opening of the bedroom door.

"Kandice, I came here to rap with you about a few things. I am not here to bring you any harm. I know that you already found the money and the papers in the floor. Let me break some of this shit down for you, Kandice,"

Virgil said as he continued to keep his arms raised so Kandice could see them.

Kandice lowered her gun and looked at the man before her. If he knew about the papers and the money in the floor, then that meant that he had knowledge about her husband or mother-in-law that she did not. She walked back into the living room and sat on the couch.

Virgil followed her into the living room and sat on the recliner across from Kandice. The two of them sized each other up as they waited for someone to speak first. Virgil smiled as he realized that the woman before him reminded him of someone else that he knew.

Virgil broke the silence and spoke first. "Kandice, what do you know about Derrick's childhood?"

Kandice pulled out a cigarette and lit it as she thought about the question. She really didn't know that much about her husband's childhood, and the thought of not knowing made her feel foolish. The smoke filled her lungs as she inhaled, and then she slowly exhaled the smoke through her nostrils.

Kandice sighed, looked at Virgil, and said, "I don't know. What should I know about his childhood?" she asked, putting the deck of cards back in his hands. She hoped that he would deal her a good spade hand in return.

Virgil asked for one of Kandice's cigarettes before he answered. Virgil knew that Kandice was in the dark, and he felt that it was his job to shed some light on her husband's background. He knew that what he was about to share with Kandice were things that even Derrick knew nothing about.

Virgie made it clear to Virgil long ago that if she died without having the opportunity to tell her baby boy all her secrets, then he was to tell Kandice with the hope that she would break the news to Derrick. Virgil understood Virgie's reasoning for wanting to tell Derrick's wife verses telling Derrick first, and he was now obligated to carry out Virgie's wishes.

"Let me tell you a story, a true story," Virgil said as he placed the cigarette to his lips and inhaled.

Kandice watched as he diverted his eyes to the window and watched the children playing in the streets. She had no idea what Virgil was talking about, but her curiosity had gotten the best of her. She sat back in the chair and waited to hear what was about to be told to her.

Virgil took the last pull from the cigarette and put it out in the ashtray. He looked at Kandice who was sitting before him. It was time to open his mouth and speak. "Kandice, you know Virgie..." he began.

Virgil then proceeded to tell Kandice information that she would have never guessed in a million years.

Kontagious

Virgil talked while Kandice listened intently to his every word. He ended the story by saying, "Now you know why Virgie couldn't tell Derrick. It's up to you how you're going to use the information."

Kandice sat there in the living room dumbfounded. She had not expected to learn so much when she entered Virgie's house that day. As she and Virgil walked out of the house, Kandice drove off with more questions than answers.

CHAPTER 11
Cheater, Cheater

"I saw you (and him and him)
Walking in the rain
You were holding hands and
I'll never be the same..."
The Rain... By: Orange Juice Jones

One Month Later...

Kandice sat at her desk in her office at her boutique, pissed. She and Derrick were supposed to meet for dinner, but she'd just hung up the phone with him after he told her that he had gotten a call from a client, and he was cancelling their dinner date.

"Lying muthafucker!" she said aloud.

Kontagious

After the conversation she'd had with Virgil, Kandice had been trying to get her marriage back on track. She and Chance were still seeing each other, and she wanted to break it off with him, but she could not find the courage to let him go. She was truly caught in a dilemma. Kandice wanted her marriage to work, but each time she was with Chance she found herself wanting to be with him more and more.As she was pondering her current triangle, her cell rang, bringing her out of her thoughts. She picked up her cell and saw the name Monica flash across the screen. Monica was Kandice's best friend

"Hey, Kandice! Whatcha doing?" Monica asked when Kandice answered.

"Girl, nothing. Sitting here fucking pissed at this nigga. But we'll talk about that later. What's good in your neck of the woods, and how is my goddaughter?" Kandice asked.

"I'm good, and Destiny is good. She's been asking me when we're going to have our girl's day out again. Anyway, I'm on my lunch break, so I really can't talk long. I was just calling to remind you to bring me your money for the cookies to the hospital before you go home."

Monica was a pediatric nurse. She and Kandice had become friends when they were in nursing school together. Kandice never completed her courses because she ended up marrying Derrick, her and Monica's friendship had endured.

"Girl, I almost forgot. How much do I owe for the Girl Scout cookies? Tell Destiny that we can get together this weekend if you're off," Kandice said as she gathered her things to head to the hospital to drop off the money.

"Well I'm glad that I called, 'cause, baby, Ms. Destiny would have had a fit if she didn't get all of the money for all the cookies that she sold. You know how she is when it comes to this shit! Anyway, you ordered five boxes, so you need to bring me twenty dollars. Just have the nurse's station page me when you get here."

The two of them talked a few minutes longer before they got off the phone. Kandice felt a little better when she hung up. Michelle always knew how to brighten her mood. As she drove to the hospital, her phone alerted her that she had a text. She smiled as she looked at the message from Chance. She typed in a quick response as she pulled into the hospital parking lot.

As she grabbed her purse and placed her hand on the door handle, Kandice had a strange premonition come over her. The feeling of dread was so overwhelming that she sat in the car with her hand on the door handle for a few seconds longer before exiting the car.

Kandice walked to the hospital's automatic door, entered, and walked to the nurse's station. Just as she was about to have one of the nurses page Monica, in her peripheral vision she saw a man who looked like Derrick sitting next to a woman in the family waiting area.

She was stuck on stupid for a minute. Kandice turned her head and squinted her eyes in the direction of the couple. Although the waiting area was dimly lit, she knew that was her husband sitting in that chair with another woman. She placed one foot in front of the other to make her way over to confront Derrick when she felt a hand being placed on her shoulder.

"Has someone helped you yet?" the woman asked.

The woman startled Kandice, but she was happy for the distraction, because she was about to get ignorant if she had made it over to where Derrick was sitting. Then an idea popped into her head.

Kandice grabbed the woman's hand that was on her shoulder and pulled her over into a corner away from the prying ears of the other nurses. The two women looked at each other, trying to figure out what the other's intentions were. Kandice took a deep breath before speaking.

"Do you want to make a quick five thousand dollars?" Kandice asked the woman.

The woman was speechless, but the mention of making some quick cash piqued her curiosity. She was in a financial bind, and the money would help her out tremendously.

"That depends on what needs to be done," the woman responded.

Kandice realized that she had the woman's attention and knew it was time to put her cards on the table. She reached inside her pursue and pulled out her wallet. She flipped through the crisp bills and pulled out ten one-hundred-dollar bills.

"This is one thousand dollars. You will get the other four thousand once you complete the task. Do you see the couple sitting in the corner in the waiting area over there?" Kandice asked.

The woman peaked her head around the corner and spotted the man and woman. Now the woman really wanted to do the job, because she figured that this was some domestic shit about to pop off. Since she loved to see drama unfold, she wanted to be there when the shit got thick.

"Yeah, so what's up? What you want me to do?" the woman asked, hoping that the young woman would fulfill her need for information.

"All I need for you to do is find out what they're doing here and as much information about why they are here. When you have that information, come to this address, ask for the owner, and I will give you the rest of your money," Kandice told her as she placed her business card with her store address on it into the woman's hand.

"If you bullshit me, you won't get shit. If you do it right, I might have another job for you at the same price," Kandice stated as she placed the money into the woman's other hand.

The woman tucked the card and the money inside her uniform before asking, "How do I know that I'm going to get the rest of my money?"

Kandice had just put one thousand dollars cash in this woman's hand, and she had the nerve to ask if Kandice was going to pay her the rest of her money? Kandice was pissed. She thought carefully before she spoke, because she did not want to piss off the chick with a smart remark. She still needed this woman to get that information for her.

"Look, you have nothing to lose. I don't know your name and you don't know mine. Besides, I just put a down payment in your hands. That should be all the reason you need to come and get the rest of your money," Kandice told her, hoping that would put an end to the questioning.

Before the woman could respond, Kandice heard a nurse calling for the parents of Derrick H. Adams Jr. Her heart sank into the pit of her stomach. Did she just hear the parents of Derrick H. Adams Jr.? That name could only mean one thing. Her husband had a fucking baby from another woman!

Both of the women watched as the couple got up and walked over to the nurse.

The woman looked at Kandice and said, "Give me a few days so that I can get as much information as possible." With those words she walked off on her fact finding expedition.

Kandice watched from the sideline as she saw Derrick and the woman talking to the nurse. She was fuming. In that one moment it became crystal clear why Derrick kept telling her that he was not ready for a baby. He wasn't ready because he already had a fucking baby! She mentally calmed down and headed for the door before her husband happened to see her. She was going to have to pay for her cookies later, because Kandice had to leave before shit got hectic in the hospital

The nurse who had called over the couple began leading them to their child's room. As she walked in front of them down the corridor, she wanted to cry. When she first saw the father's name, she had suspicions, but she had to see the father's face and eyes to confirm her thoughts. When she laid her eyes on him, her suspicions were confirmed. But this was not the right time nor place for her to voice what she knew was the truth. She was there to do her job, and she would have to deal with her demons later.

They made it to the room where Derrick Jr. was resting. Another nurse stood in front of the child as she wrote on his medical chart. The nurse completed her notes, smiled at them, and exited.

Derrick and Alexis faced the nurse who had accompanied them into their child's room. The nurse smiled warmly when she saw the worry on their faces. She reviewed her chart notes and was pleased to read that the child was going to be just fine.

"Mr. and Mrs. Adams, my name is Nurse Charlotte Jackson. From the tests that were run on your son, it appears that he has as stomach virus. He's sleeping right now but he will be fine in a few days; once the virus passes through his body. The doctor will be in shortly to release him. Your son will be fine," she told them with a pleasant smile, although her soul was crying on the inside.

Charlotte then turned and walked out the door, leaving the parents to be with their child. As she walked down the hospital's hallway and headed to the ladies' room, she felt tears begin to well in her eyes.

Kandice had been sitting in her Range Rover waiting for her husband to walk out of the hospital. She had been there waiting for almost an hour. She had many thoughts going through her head and feelings rushing through her body, but the one thing that she was not feeling was remorse. Seeing Derrick with another woman and finding out that he had a child was all the vindication that she needed to continue her infidelity.

As her thoughts became clearer, she realized that she was in a parking lot full of cars and had no idea where Derrick's car was parked. Kandice looked at her cell phone to check the time. She waited a few minutes longer and then pushed the OnStar icon in her car."This is OnStar. How can I help you?" the OnStar representative asked as her voice boomed through the speakers in the SUV.

"Yes, my husband and I are out, and we seem to can't find his vehicle in the parking lot. Can you locate his car and send the location to the GPS in my car?" Kandice asked.

The rep typed in a few things into the system and returned back with the information. "Ms. Adams, it seems that your other vehicle is located at 1500 Courtdale Street. Do you need me to send you a map to the location?" the rep asked.

Kandice now knew that Derrick's car was not at the hospital, which meant that his car had to be parked at his baby's mother's house. She turned on her car and answered, "Yes, send me the directions."

Kontagious

The OnStar rep sent the directions to Kandice's car's GPS and Kandice pulled off. As she followed the directions, she began to plot. She was formulating a plan that was sure to add to her fury.

Kandice pulled up on the block and spotted Derrick's metallic silver Cadillac CTS-V sedan parked under a street light in front of an expensive apartment complex. The gate was open and the security guard on duty was fast asleep in the security booth. Kandice casually pulled her Range through the open gate, parked in the cut under a tree directly in sight of Derrick's car, cut off her car, and waited. She was wide awake because on her way over to the address she stopped at Starbucks and picked up a Grande Carmel Macchiato.

She looked at her stereo and the time read three-thirty pm. Kandice turned up the volume on her stereo and bopped her head to the lyrics of the old school mix coming through the speakers. As she was singing along, her cell phone rang. She looked at the screen and saw that it was Derrick. Kandice allowed the call to go to voicemail and continued to keep her eyes open for any car pulling up.

Derrick, Alexis, and DJ were driving in Alexis's baby Benz when he called his wife. He figured that she must be pissed because he'd cancelled their plans for the night, and he wanted to check in on her. When Alexis had called informing him that DJ was running a fever and vomiting that she was taking him to the hospital, he'd rushed over there, dropped off his car, and they'd headed to the hospital together.

He was thankful that his son was only suffering from a stomach virus, but he knew now that he was going to have to tell his wife about his baby's mother and child. Derrick loved DJ beyond anything in the world and he was determined to be a good father to him, but he also wanted to stay married to Kandice.

The ride back to Alexis's apartment was short and the three of them were tired from being in the hospital for several hours. Derrick knew that he needed to get his car and go home when he got there, but when DJ asked if he was staying the night, he couldn't find it in his heart to tell his son no. Derrick turned left onto Courtdale Street and rode down the street until he was pulling into the apartment complex's parking lot.

He pulled the Benz next to his Caddy and got out. Right after he exited the car Alexis got out with DJ in her arms. When Derrick saw that she was carrying DJ, he quickly walked over to her and grabbed his son from her arms. Alexis placed their son in Derrick's arms, and then leaned in and kissed Derrick.

Kandice saw the Benz pull into the parking lot and park next to Derrick's car. She paid close attention and watched her husband play happy family with his baby's mother and child. Her eyes didn't even blink when she saw them kiss. Kandice watched the whole scene play out right before her eyes and instead of crying, a smile crept across her face, and then she busted out in laughter. Her laughter continued as she cranked up her SUV and headed back to her house. She was hysterically laughing because as she was watching her husband with the next bitch an ironic song came on the radio. Kandice turned the song up to the max in the car and started singing.

"I saw you (and him and him) walking in the rain. You were holding hands, and I'll never be the same..."

CHAPTER 12
Time for a Change

"Fast livin' got me trapped in this street game
Before I die I hope I have a chance to make a change
I'm at the time in my life when a nigga ready to change
I'll be dead or in jail if I don't shake this thang
feel like I'm trapped in a prison, slowly waiting to die..."
If I Could Change... Master P

Chance drove a navy blue 1990 Ford Taurus on his way to what he called his product house. One of his carriers had just brought a shipment up from the bottom. As he crept through the streets he thought back to his earlier days in the game.

When he first got in the game he was selling that white candy, but when he started to see the white kids getting high off popping pills, he saw a gold mine in the making. After some extensive investigation into the world of pill popping, he found out that the pills got the addict higher and he could sell them for more money than cocaine.

He hooked up with a doctor in North Florida who was willing to sell him all the prescription drugs that he needed, and that was the beginning of the product house. His operation was complicated, but yet simple. Chance was a planner and had done his research before he put his master plan into action. Before he, J-Rock, and Quinton opened up shop, Chance laid out how the operation was going to function.

The first thing they did was put their money together and opened up three small corner stores. The stores were deeded in the names of deceased people. Each store was located in close proximity to a predominantly white high school, a predominantly white technical college, and a predominantly white four-year university. After the stores were up and running, the small trio implemented Operation Loodie Doodie.

Chance had a seven step plan.

Step 1: Buy one-thousand-dollars of burner cell phones

Step 2: Spread the word that they were open for business

Step 3: When people wanted to buy pills, they would send a text to one of the burners, and then a return text was sent giving the buyer an address for where to pay

Step 4: Once the money was exchanged, the buyer was given another address and a code word, and the seller snapped a photo of the buyer.

Step 5: The picture was sent via text to another burner at the store where the customer was headed to pick up the product

Step 6: When buyers made it to the store, they gave the code word and their identities were verified by the photos.

Step 7: After the buyer's identity was confirmed, he was led to the bathroom where the product was produced, and then he was rushed out the back door of the store.

Chance and his inner circle never touched the product. There was never any money and product exchanged at the same time, and if they ever felt funny about a person trying to buy from them, the deal was never made. None of the buyers knew their names, and none of them could ever say that Chance or his boys sold pills to them directly. Every few weeks they changed the burners and would pay someone to spread the word with the new numbers.

Kontagious

The reason for doing business in three different locations was because one store sold only Oxy, Percocet, and other opiates. The second store sold Ritalin, Adderall, and other stimulants, and the third location sold a mixture of both stimulants and opiates. They sold pills from ten dollars per pill all the way up to fifty dollars. The average customer was buying one-hundred-dollars worth of pills each day, and each of the stores did around two hundred sales per day, which meant that Chance, J-Rock, and Quinton split four hundred twenty thousand dollars each week.

After almost five years dealing in pills, Chance had amassed a great deal of wealth. Now it was time to make his move out of the game. He was ready to find a woman that was down to ride with him, make her his wife, and have some babies that would carry on his legacy.

As he continued to drive to the product house, his phone rang. He was happy to see that it was Kandice calling. He answered just as he pulled up to his destination.

"What's up? I was just thinking about you," Chance said as he placed the car into park.

Kandice smiled at the sound of his voice. She wanted to see him, but she knew that she would have to bide her time for a hot minute until she figured out how she was going to get out of her marriage and crush her husband.

But for now she placed those thoughts on the back burner and concentrated on her boo.

"Oh, you were? Hmmm, what were you thinking?" she asked as she envisioned him licking her hot juices.

Chance licked his lips as Kandice's sexy tone graced his ear. He wanted to have a nice phone sex convo with her, but he was on time constraints.

"Baby, I'm glad to hear your voice, but we gonna have to cut this conversation short until the morning. But, check this, there is something that I want to talk to you about. So when I call you tomorrow, make room in your schedule to see me," Chance told her.

Kandice was quiet as she listened to Chance. She was curious about what he wanted to tell her and she wanted to know right then, but she already knew there was no pushing Chance. She was going to have to wait until he was ready to tell her.

"All right, boo, call me when you get the chance. I'm trying to see you too. Talk to you later," Kandice said, then ended the call.

Chance sat in the car a few minutes longer. He checked his surroundings to make sure that the street was isolated and that no one had followed him. As he exited the car and headed inside the house, he thought, *I've been living this fast life too long. It's time to make a change.*

ACT IV

CHAPTER 13
Riding the Pony

If your horny, Let's do it
Ride it, My Pony
My saddle's waiting
Come and jump on it

If your horny, Let's do it
Ride it, My Pony
My saddle's waiting
Come and jump on it…
Pony By: Ginuwine

Derrick was licking and sucking feverishly on Kandice's clit as if he was truly sorry for something that he had done. The truth of the matter was that Derrick was trying to fuck his wife so good to conceal his guilt for living a double life.

"Damn, boy, you about to make me cum again!" Kandice said as she felt her body beginning to shake from her third orgasm.

She grabbed the back of her husband's head and thrust her wide hips farther onto his tongue. Kandice was in a state of sexual bliss as she enjoyed receiving head from the man that she was now plotting against. In a quick motion she swung her leg over Derrick's head and got on all fours. Her hands found Derrick's chest as she forced his body down onto the bed.

"Give me this dick!" Kandice said as she straddled his hardened dick.

She mounted him and began to give the performance of a lifetime. Kandice put all of her energy into riding him. Unbeknownst to him, she was trying to conceal her guilt too. However, her guilt was not from cheating, but from knowing that Derrick was unaware of what she was engineering against him. She only felt guilt, because she knew that her plotting was going to blindside Derrick. As the thoughts of seeking revenge turned from guilt into the feeling of getting satisfaction.

"Whose dick is this? Talk to me, daddy!" Kandice demanded.

Derrick was in his own world. Kandice's pussy was so wet and the suction from her juices was dripping down his shaft. He placed his hands on her hips and guided her farther down onto his dick. "Damn, this your dick!" he said as he smacked her on her ass.

Kandice turned around and rode him like a black stallion. Her bouncing motions caused them both to climax simultaneously. Although she was sweating profusely, she was still horny for more. She jumped off the dick, got on her knees, and let her mouth taste the mixture of her and Derrick's juices. As she was on her knees, her eyes found her husband's eyes, and they locked eyes for a moment. Derrick's eyes showed great remorse while Kandice's eyes hid her vengeance and his demise. The sucking sounds coming from Kandice's mouth finally caused Derrick to close his eyes as his body succumbed to the pleasure.

Kandice smiled as she continued to suck his dick. *Yeah, nigga, I'm gonna ride your pony right to your downfall,* she thought.

CHAPTER 14
Computer Love

Shooby doo bop shoo doo bop I wanna love you
Shooby doo bop [I wanna love you, baby] computer love
Shooby doo bop shoo doo bop I wanna love you
Shooby doo bop my computer love…
Computer Love… By: Zapp & Roger

Kandice stood at the cash register waiting for her employee Marshane to come through the door. Kandice had finally found the answer to the missing monies in her accounts, and that answer was Marshane.

The day she discovered that someone was misappropriating her money; Kandice immediately took action by beginning her own investigation. She visited the local spy store and purchased a Spy-Stik and a camera to observe what was transpiring in and around the cash register. When she'd retrieved the information from the camera and Spy-Stik, she was shocked to find out that Marshane was the one hacking into her bank accounts. The pictures from the camera showed exactly how Marshane was able to steal Kandice's money. Kandice had to admit that Marshane's technique was slick, but no one was slicker than Kandice.

Kandice had every intention of firing Marshane when she first discovered her employee's betrayal, but when she saw how good Marshane was at what she'd done, Kandice knew she could utilize Marshane's talents in other ways. After seeing Derrick with his baby's mother and child, the gifts that Marshane possessed were ones that she could not let slip away.

"Hey, Ms. Kandice! How are you?" a cheery Marshane asked as she entered the boutique and made her way to the cash register to clock in.

Before Kandice could engage Marshane in a conversation, the bells from the front door chimed, alerting them that a customer had entered the store. The woman walked in and Marshane was about to greet her when Kandice cut her off.

"It's OK, Marshane. She and I have a standing appointment. I will be in my office for a while."

Kandice and the customer walked toward the back of the store and into Kandice's office. Once the door was closed, Kandice locked it and sat in her executive chair. The woman appeared to be anxious, but Kandice put her at ease. "Look, there is no need to be scared. I have your money. Do you have my information?"

The woman sat back in the chair that was directly in front of the mahogany desk. She liked Kandice's swagger and confidence. She had to smile at the air of arrogance that Kandice exuded. The woman reached inside her Coach purse and pulled out her Verizon smartphone.

Kandice watched closely as the woman scrolled down the screen until she found what she was searching for. The woman looked up from her phone's screen display and said, "I was able to get more than enough information on your couple. Technology is a bitch when you doing dirt," she said as she handed over her phone.

Kandice grabbed the phone and looked at what was displayed on the screen. She raised her eyebrows as she read the contents. The woman had just handed over photo images of the child's medical file, insurance information, and medical information about her husband and the child's mother.

Kandice opened a desk drawer and pulled out a universal USB phone cord from the top drawer of her desk. She placed the USB cord into the phone and transferred the images from the phone to her laptop computer. Once the images were fully downloaded and placed into a file, she handed the cell phone back to the woman.

"Can you do another job for me?" Kandice asked as she pulled out her wallet.

The woman watched as Kandice counted out forty Benjamin Franklins and held them in her hand as she waited for a response. The woman thought for several seconds longer before answering.

"Yes," the woman responded. "But before I venture into this this next job I need to know who I'm getting into bed with. I see that your money is good, but it would be nice to know what I should call you. Let me start by saying... my name... well... uh... just call me Lisa."

Kandice extended her hand and replied, "You can call me Kontagious." The two women shook hands and then the business of Lisa's next assignment was discussed.

The two women talked in length about what Kandice wanted. Once their business meeting was concluded, Kandice paid Lisa five thousand dollars—the four thousand that she owed for the first job, and a one-thousand-dollar deposit on the next job.

Kandice walked Lisa to the front door, and once she was gone, Kandice stood in front of the store's door, thinking. It was now time for Kandice to confront Marshane about what she'd done.

"Marshane, what are you in school for again?" Kandice asked as she stood in front of the register with her arms folded.

Marshane stopped what she was doing and looked at her boss. She immediately knew that something wasn't right. Then her conscience started to fuck with her about what she had been doing. Although she felt guilty about what she had done, Marshane could not allow her true feelings to show as she stood face to face with the woman from whom she'd been stealing.

"I'm a computer science major. Why do you ask?" Marshane asked.

Marshane's answer made it crystal clear to Kandice how the young woman had learned to hack into computers. Kandice was impressed that a black girl from the hood was able to master skills that were thought to be something only young, white kids were capable of understanding.

Kandice shook her head and proceeded with her line of questioning, "Computer science major? So what exactly can you do with this type of degree?" Kandice was just asking these bullshit ass questions to try to scare Marshane.

When Kandice asked that next question, Marshane's hood instinct kicked in full throttle. Marshane had a quick flashback and she distinctly remembered having a previous conversation with Kandice about her major. She knew that Kandice had an almost photographic memory, so if Kandice was asking these questions, then Marshane was busted.

Marshane was the first person in her immediate family to attend college. She had high hopes of graduating and opening up her own computer firm specializing in Internet security. However, when one of her classmates turned her on to how to use her knowledge of the inner workings of computers and computer programming to hack into computers, she'd practiced and become a pro. She was confident that her hacking skills were of a superior caliber. Now she was wondering how Kandice had caught on to what she had done.

The money that she'd stolen from Kandice was money that she needed for her family to survive. Her mother was terminally ill and she was the oldest of three siblings. Embezzling money had become her hustle. Now she was in fear that Kandice was about to press criminal charges on her for her crime.

Kandice saw the terror in Marshane's eyes. She knew that the young girl now realized that she was busted. Kandice didn't want Marshane to flee the store since she had a proposal to make, so she quickly tried to calm Marshane.

"Marshane, don't run. I am not going to press charges. Keep the money. I want to hire you for your hacking services," Kandice told her employee as she placed a hand on her shoulder.

Marshane began to hyperventilate because she was still afraid. She figured that Kandice was playing on her intelligence. Marshane made a quick decision—haul ass! She pushed Kandice's hand off her shoulder and with the other hand she grabbed her purse.

She took off toward the store's door, but she was stopped by Kandice's quick speed. Marshane had no idea that Kandice was a former track star. The two ladies met once again at the store's front door.

Kandice slapped the shit out of Marshane and pulled her by the arm back over to the register. Kandice gripped Marshane by both of her arms and looked her square in her eyes. "Look, I already told you that I'm not going to press charges! I want you to do some work for me. If you do this for me and do it right, I will give you another fifty K for your troubles," Kandice stated.

The mention of money was all that Marshane needed to hear. She needed the money for school and her family. Marshane would do anything to provide for the ones she loved the most in the world. Her only question was why.

Why was Kandice not charges if she knew that Marshane had stolen her money?

"If you know what I did, why are you not pressing charges and firing me?" Marshane asked.

Kandice released her grip on Marshane's arms. She hoped that the girl remained calm. She took two steps back, because if the young lady got buck and decided to swing, she wanted to be at the right distance to jab Marshane dead in her face.

"I'm not pressing charges because the evidence that I have on you reflects that you are good, if not great at what you do," Kandice responded. "I have my own personal reasons for wanting to hire your services, but my word is my bond.

"The fifty K that you stole, keep it. I will give you another fifty K to do a job for me. However, if you steal one more penny from any of my accounts, not only will I press charges, but I will petition the court to send you far away from your family so it will be difficult for them to see you. You can decline my offer, walk out of the store, and consider yourself fired, but I really need you to do this job."

The mention of being sent to a prison that was far away from her mother and siblings caused Marshane's heart to ache. She and Kandice had never had any type of ill feelings toward each other, and Marshane felt confident that Kandice was always true to her word.

Marshane placed her purse on the counter and pulled out her laptop. As the machine booted up, she looked at Kandice. The two women stood side by side and watched the Windows screen pop up. Marshane typed in her encrypted code and her computer settings loaded, not looking like anything that Kandice had seen before.

Kandice walked to the store's door and locked it. They were closed for the day as far as she was concerned. The job she had for Marshane was one that was long and complicated. They walked into Kandice's office. For the next few hours Kandice ran down to Marshane exactly what she needed from her. Marshane confirmed that she would have no problem hacking into the computers and companies that Kandice mentioned.

After Kandice finished detailing what she needed, she gave Marshane a five-thousand-dollar good faith deposit and sent her home. Once Kandice was alone in the store, she opened one of her desk drawers and pulled out a Cuban cigar and a flask. She lit the cigar and took a swig from the flask. Before she took another sip, she raised the flask toward the ceiling and said, "Information, technology, and hacking—what a deadly combination." Her plan for revenge had begun.

CHAPTER 15
Work to do

"I'm taking care of business, baby can't you see
I gotta make it for you, and I gotta make it for me
Sometimes it may seem girl I'm neglecting you
I'd love to spend more time
But I got so many things to do..."
The Isley Brothers… Work to Do

Lisa made her way home after leaving the boutique. Her mind kept thinking about the name Kontagious had mentioned in their meeting. She knew the name was familiar to her from somewhere.

When she walked inside her house she immediately wished she had somewhere else to go. Lisa was married to a man who was both mentally and physically abusive. The main reason she took the job from Kontagious was because she was getting her money up so she could leave her husband. After being married since the age of eighteen and finally finding the courage to leave ten years later, it was a blessing in disguise when she was offered the money from Kontagious.

"Where the fuck you been at?" were the first words that Lisa's husband said when she entered the house.

Lisa placed her purse on the table and walked into the living room where her husband waited for her. When she entered the room and the sight of her husband made her want to vomit, Lisa knew it was definitely time for her to go. She almost had enough money to make her move, and this last job for Kontagious was going to be the butter on top of the bread.

"I had to make a stop before I came home," Lisa responded.

Her husband looked at her and his disposition went from calm to irate. He jumped up from the couch and leaped over the coffee table to stand directly in front of Lisa. His nostrils flared from his heavy breathing.

"You stopped to see your nigga before you came home to your husband!" he yelled.

Before Lisa could defend herself, his hand wrapped firmly around her neck and he began to apply pressure. The look in his eyes as he squeezed her neck was one of insanity. Lisa placed her tiny hands around his hand and attempted to pull his hand away from her windpipe. After what seemed like an eternity, he released his hand from Lisa's neck.

When she was able to grasp for air she placed her hand around her neck and inhaled the air as it re-entered into her body. Lisa had become so use to this type of abuse that she was surprised that she was not dead yet. As Lisa's breathing pattern slowly returned to normal, she began to hear her inner voice speaking to her. The voice told her that this was it. It was time for her to leave right now. The voice told her plain as day to attack and get the hell out of the house.

Because she and her husband were standing so close to each other, when she lifted her knee at full force, it connected with his dick. He slumped over in pain, grabbing his dick.

Lisa saw that he was in pain and she continued her attack. She raised her foot and stomped him in his face. Her foot connected with his face so many times that he didn't know whether to place his hands up to his face or guard his dick. When she got tired of stomping his face, she raised the other foot and began stomping his chest and ribs. She was actually getting pleasure from inflicting the same pain on him that he had inflicted on her for so many years. Lisa continued to administer an ass whooping to her husband that lasted for well over forty-five minutes.

Meanwhile...

Marshane sat in what she called her lab. It was a small studio where she had set up various computers. For the last six months she had been trying her hacking skills on a larger scale by tapping into certain businesses' computer systems. As she was getting into the groove preparing for her next project with Kandice, her cell phone vibrated, letting her know that she had a text.

She had been waiting on Kandice to text her so Marshane could obtain one of the computer's IP addresses that Kandice had requested she hack. Kandice's text read: Bout to start the chat in one min. Be ready.

Marshane opened her online chat application and waited for Kandice to find her. "This is going to be fun!" Marshane said as the icon popped up asking her if she wanted to chat with D_Adams. After Marshane accepted, Kandice typed: What do you need me to do?"

Hold on. I almost got it, Marshane typed.

Marshane typed in a few codes and instantly she was able to pull up the IP address for the computer where Kandice was logged in.

I got what I need. Keep the computer on and make sure it's online. I should have all that I need within thirty minutes. Will text you and tell you to turn off the computer., Marshane typed.

Back at Lisa's house...

Lisa had beaten her husband unconscious. She had finally found the courage to fight him back. After grabbing the baseball bat that was in the house, she proceeded to beat him with it. The last blow was square to his dome, which caused him to pass out.

She was running through the house gathering a few things and throwing them into a bag when she heard a phone ringing. The ringtone was unfamiliar to her, and she didn't see a phone, so she followed the sound. When she reached the bedroom the ringing got louder and she could tell it was coming from underneath her bed. She got on her knees and felt around until she retrieved a shoebox.

When she opened the box she saw a wad of cash and a cell phone. She looked at the screen and the name that flashed across it was Alexis. Lisa saw the name and became hot! She had not once been unfaithful to her husband, but the nigga was fucking another bitch! She grabbed the cash and left the phone on the bed.

Lisa walked back into the living room where she saw her husband trying to regain consciousness. She picked up the bat once again and swung with all her might, hitting him in his ribcage. She heard a crack and realized that her blow had broken one or more of his ribs. Her husband screamed.

She quickly picked up her bag with clothes, her purse, and the wad of cash, and walked out the door. She knew that she had to lay low because her husband was bound to kill her for sure when he found her. Lisa planned on finishing the job for Kontagious and leaving the city for good. Lisa saw a cab pulling up on her street, she signaled for him to pull over and she got in. Her destination was unclear, but she knew it was far away from where she was now. She told the cab driver to drive.

The driver pulled off and turned the volume up on the old school radio station. The song that came on next was The Isley Brothers: Work to Do… the funny thing was two other women… Kontangious and Marshane were both listening to the same station hearing the same song… it was as if the three of them were all on one accord they all had work to do.

CHAPTER 16
Where The Party At?

If the party's where your at just let me know
Don't be trippin when you see us in the club
Just show a little love, represent your side like me
'Cause 'round here if you slick you pick a hot one
Ride shotgun, couple of 'em got one
Belvedere in the rear of the club
Pulled up on dubs and we 'bout to go and buy the bar up
So So, for sure we ain't playin
Hang with no lames, hit the park and sayin...
Ay, where the party at?
Girls is on the way, where the Bacardi at?
Models and models, talkin all a that
Know I can't forget about my thugs
(Where the party at?)
And all my girls
(Where the party at?)

Kontagious

Off in the club
(Where the party at?)
If the party's where you're at let me hear you say
Uh ooooooooooooh
(uh oh oh oh)
Uh ooooooooooooh
(uh oh oh oh)
Uh ooooooooooooh
(uh oh oh oh)
Uh ooooooooooooh
If the party's where you're at just let me know…
Where The Party At… By: Jagged Edge

A few weeks after Alexis's initial meeting with
Chance, Quinton, and J-Rock, Chance advised her that he
wanted in on the real estate venture with Empire. To
celebrate Chance's retirement and his entry into the legit
real estate game, Chance was throwing a party. J-Rock
had invited Alexis to the party, but she wanted to confirm
the time and location, so she tried calling him. When he
didn't answer, she left a voice mail.

As Alexis sat at her desk working, she waited for
Derrick to return from running an errand. He was her
partner at Empire Real Estate Brokerage, LLC, and had
asked her to stay at work until he returned. At that
moment Alexis heard someone enter the reception area.
Hoping it was Derrick, she looked through her glass door
and saw an unexpected visitor entering.

CHAPTER 17
Power of the P-U-S-S-Y

The power of the P-U-S-S-Y,
Thatz why every mutherfucka in the world dress fly.
Every baller that can afford it they cop the best ride, for
the power of the P-U-S-S-Y. (Let's have some fun)
The power of the P-U-S-S-Y, thatz why niggaz get they
hair cut, try to dress fly. Every baller that can afford it he
cop the best ride. For the Power of the P-U-S-S-Y...
Pussy... By: Jay-Z

Kandice walked through the doors of Empire Real
Estate Brokerage, LLC, her husband's business. She was
not usually involved in his business dealings and rarely
visited him at his office, but today she was there on a
mission. She needed certain information in order to take
the next step in her plan for revenge.

Kontagious

She spoke to the receptionist who advised Kandice that Derrick was not in. That was fine with Kandice. She didn't give a fuck where he was. She told the receptionist that she would wait for her husband inside his office. As she turned on her heel and started toward his office, Alexis stepped out from her office. Kandice had to play it cool, although she was 100 percent sure that Alexis was Derrick's baby's mother. Although, Virgil had neglected to inform her about her husband's love child, she wasn't mad, because the wealth of information that he gave her was better than she could have imagined.

"Hi, Alexis, how are you?" Kandice asked, not really giving a fuck.

"I'm good. What about you?" Alexis asked, curious about why Kandice was at the office.

"Good. Just here to see my husband. By the way, Derrick told me the other day that your son was having a birthday soon. I didn't know you had a baby. I would love to buy him something," Kandice said with a fake smile plastered on her face, knowing that her words were fucking with Alexis.

Alexis was caught off guard by the comment about her son. She knew that Derrick had not told Kandice about their child, and she also knew that he would not arbitrarily divulge information about DJ. Kandice was coming at her from some angle, but she had no clue from which one. However, she was good at poker, and she was not about to let Kandice know that she was surprised by her comments.

"Huumph, well I had no idea that my boss was that involved in his employees' lives. But, yes, my son will be having a birthday soon." Before she could finish speaking, Kandice's cell rang.

"Excuse me, I have to take this call," Kandice said as she continued toward Derrick's office. "It was nice speaking with you."

Alexis watched as her child's father's wife walked down the hall. She was livid on the inside with jealously. Alexis was convinced that she deserved to have Derrick's last name, not Kandice, especially since she was the mother of Derrick's son! After that conversation, she was done with work for the day. She grabbed her purse and car keys, and headed out the door to see her son.

Kandice entered Derrick's office, closed the door behind her, and then closed her cell phone. Marshane had called to tell her that she was ready whenever Kandice was. Kandice sat behind Derrick's desk and moved the mouse. To her surprise, he'd left his computer unlocked and running. She searched for a chat application to contact Marshane, but when she did not see one, she navigated to Yahoo and began downloading Yahoo messenger.

Kontagious

As the application downloaded, Kandice became panicked. She was not sure when Derrick would return to his office, and she didn't want to be caught red-handed doing her dirt. Finally the download completed and she and Marshane connected.

It appears that all of the computers in the office are linked together, Marshane typed. It will take at least an hour for me to get all the information.

Kandice read the message and sighed. Just when she was about to type in her response, the door opened and Derrick walked in. She quickly exited from the chat box. She and her husband looked at each other. Kandice smiled and said, "Hey, baby! I wanted to come see you!"

She rose from the chair and strutted over to her husband, placing her arms around his neck.

"Hello to you too! If I had known that you were coming by, I would have made a lunch reservation for us," Derrick said as he kissed her on the cheek.

Derrick made his way to his desk and sat in his chair. He noticed that his computer was on, but he couldn't remember if he'd locked it before he'd left. There was shit on his computer that he didn't need Kandice to see, so he hoped he hadn't fucked up.

Kandice easily read her husband's facial expressions and could tell that he was thinking about the computer.

She needed to distract him and take away all of his concerns so Marshane could get what she needed, so Kandice walked over to the desk chair and straddled her husband.

"I hope you don't mind, but I was web surfing," Kandice said as her tongue slithered up his earlobe. She knew that was his spot, and it would not be long before they were on the floor getting it on.

"Girl, you know that's my spot. What you doing?" Derrick asked as he felt his pipe become hard as steel.

Kandice did not reply. Instead she turned her head and saw that he'd left the door wide open. She got up, closed the office door, and locked it. Then she turned to face her husband and slowly unbuttoned her shirt, showing him her perky 32C breasts. Once her shirt was unfastened, she pulled her right breast out of her bra and placed her mouth on her nipple.

She slowly sucked her brown nipple, causing her pussy to secrete her sweet juices inside her panties. As she continued to stimulate herself, she wiggled out of her pants and exposed her matching underwear. Then Kandice turned around so that her ass was in direct view of Derrick's eyes, and she smacked her ass cheek. The sound from the slap reverberated throughout the office.

Derrick sat quietly enjoying his private strip tease. His dick was rock solid as it patiently waited to enter his wife's cave. Derrick grabbed his dick and gently squeezed his throbbing shaft.

"Come over here and ride daddy's dick!" Derrick demanded as he unzipped his pants and pulled out his solider from the confines of his boxers.

Kandice heard his command, but she wasn't yet done with her show. She finished undressing and let her hands roam freely until her hand slid to her lower lips. Her fingers spread her lips until her forefinger found her center.

"Hmmmm!" she moaned as her finger moved in and out of her pink opening.

Kandice enjoyed seeing the lust in her husband's eyes. Times like this made her wish that she wasn't plotting on him. Although she was well aware of his love child, she still loved her husband. But her feelings of love had become overshadowed with feelings of hurt, distrust, and retribution.

"You like that, daddy? You like it when this pussy is nice and wet for you, don't you?" Kandice teased.

The masturbation show went on for a few more minutes until her finger could no longer satisfy her. She walked closer to Derrick's chair and resumed her position on his lap. Her freshly manicured hand grabbed his dick and stroked it until the veins on the side were pulsating.

She lifted her body and came down on his dick, triggering them both to moan in unison.

"Got damn! This pussy is good!" Derrick muttered as he felt Kandice's walls contract around his dick.

She slowly lifted her hips and slid back down the pipe. Kandice was enjoying having him inside her. She wanted this last time that they made love to be enjoyable for both of them, because after this time, Derrick was never going to be inside her again. She grabbed her breasts and placed her nipples inside his mouth.

Derrick flicked his tongue on each of her brown nipples. His mouth sucked on each of her breasts as if he was a baby breast feeding. But he had to stop his sucking when Kandice started winding on his dick, making him feel as if he was having an epileptic seizure.

Still inside of her, Derrick picked up Kandice and placed her in his chair. He wasn't ready to bust yet, and he wanted to fuck her until she couldn't take it anymore. Derrick pulled out of her and pushed back the chair. He bent down so his body fit under the desk. Then he lowered his head and began to unleash a tonguing to her clit. The wetness from her pussy was plastered on his chin, but he didn't give a fuck. He was caught in the moment. Kandice palmed his head and pushed Derrick's mouth farther onto her spot. She closed her eyes and images of Chance flashed inside her mind. She was on the verge of calling out his name, but she opened her eyes and remembered that the man between her legs was not her lover, but her husband.

Kandice felt her body on the verge of nutting in Derrick's mouth. She pumped his face faster and gyrated her hips to the pace of his tongue.

"Ohhhh... shit!" she shouted as she palmed the back of his head and allowed her cum to flow inside his mouth. To her surprise he continued to eat her as if he was never going to have another meal in his life.

The wetness from his mouth and tongue began to drive her up the wall. She wanted him to stop and she tried to move her body away from his mouth, but to no avail. Derrick pulled her back toward his mouth. To make sure that she was going to sit there and take the pleasure, Derrick placed her legs around his neck and continued to feast.

"You 'bout to make me cum again! Damn, you eating this pussy!" Kandice whimpered.

Derrick ignored her pleas and continued on his mission to please his wife. He felt her body tense up and then release in his mouth and on his face. He licked her center a few more times and was satisfied that he had given Kandice sexual gratification.

Derrick got up from under the desk, pulled down his pants, and stepped out of them. Then he grabbed his dick and stroked it, making it expand to its full length. Placing Kandice's legs around his waist, he plunged inside her pussy.

He long stroked her until she begged him to fuck her brains out. His dick slid in and out of her pussy as his balls smacked against her thigh. Derrick pumped like a mad man and was ready bust his seed. He removed her legs from his waist, lowered them, pulled her hips closer, and turned her around so that she was face down and ass up.

Derrick placed both of his hands on Kandice's ass cheeks and smacked them. Her ass bounced like jelly as his dick found the core of her love, which was soaking wet. He pushed forward as his nine inches of hard dick rammed faster inside the pussy.

"Damn, this pussy is good! You ready for this dick, girl? I'm 'bout to bust off in you!" Derrick grunted as he smacked her ass again for dramatic effect. He then pulled all the way out and dug back inside Kandice. With that final dive, his seed spilled inside her wet cave.

The sweat from their bodies dripped onto the floor as they both tried to catch their breaths. They were exhausted. Derrick pulled his limp dick out of Kandice and stepped away from her. He looked at her and marveled at the flawlessness of her body.

Kontagious

"Kandice, you got a nigga tired as fuck now!" Derrick said as he let out a laugh.

Kandice turned her body around and stood before her husband. She leaned in and kissed his lips. They kissed like two high school kids. When she came up for air, she winked at him, then walked over to where her clothes were flung across the floor.

"You know why you tired," she said as she put on her underwear. "It's because I got the power of the pussy! When the pussy snaps down on you, it depletes you of your energy! You ain't know?" she asked, and they both laughed at her smart ass comment.

After they finished getting dressed, they began to head out the door. Kandice looked around the office to make sure that she had all of her belongings. She saw her cell phone on Derrick's desk and grabbed it. As soon as the phone was firmly in the palm of her hand, it beeped, indicating that she had a text. She looked at the text and saw that she had two missed text messages, both from Marshane.

She quickly read the texts. The first one said, Almost done, and the second one said, Finished. Meet me at the store in two hours. Kandice placed her phone inside her purse and walked out the door behind her husband. That day's mission was accomplished. All the pieces to her plan were definitely coming together.

ACT V

CHAPTER 18
The 411

Here's the dirt
Extra, extra, read all about it
(Extra, extra, read all about it)
We got the beat and we gonna shout it
(We got the beat and we gonna shout it)

We got down to the parlor, it was rough, raw
Said you gotta do somethin stead of nothin at all
Because there's people you desire, people you admire
You wanna go places fore you get too tired

We want the truth about what's been goin on
So we chitter chatter, gossip on our telephone
Well, now our time is running out, we ain't got forever
Everybody wants a piece of lifelong pleasure
Oh, yeah, yeah
Headlines
(Read all about it)
Headlines

(Headlines)
It's in the streets…
Headlines… By: MidnightStar

Kandice pulled up to the boutique and walked inside. To her astonishment Marshane and Lisa were both waiting for her.

"I hope you don't mind, but when I got here she was waiting outside for you, so I let her in and I told her that you would be here shortly," Marshane explained. "Naw, you good. I'm glad that both of you are here anyway. So let me meet with Lisa first, and when I'm done we can talk."

Kandice tapped Lisa on her shoulder and told her to follow her back to her office. As the two of them walked to the back, Kandice could see that Lisa was visibly upset and agitated. Her disposition made Kandice concerned. She opened her office door and ushered Lisa inside.

Lisa sat down in front of Kandice's desk, and Kandice sat in her desk chair. There was a brief silence, then Kandice broke it by asking, "What's up with you? You seem a bit stressed. Anything you want to talk about?"

Lisa dropped her head in shame. She was officially on the run from her husband. She had gotten the information that she needed, put in a resignation letter to the hospital effective immediately, booked a flight, and was now there to collect her payment. She was ready to leave. One thing she was certain of was that J-Rock would surely kill her if she didn't get ghost, and soon.

"No, I'm good. I just need to get my money and get out of town. Here's a copy of everything that I could find. The funny thing is I kept telling myself that the name sounded familiar, and I came to find out that she's one of the nurses at the hospital where I worked. The file is big because I did some extensive digging and I was able to find the birth records for her children. " Lisa handed over a manila folder of photocopied papers.

Kandice walked over to the copier in her office and made another set of copies of the documents Lisa provided. When the copies were done, she placed one set inside her safe and pulled out the remainder of Lisa's money. Then she returned to her seat and placed the other set inside her purse.

"Thank you," Kandice said. "You have been more help than you will ever know, but tell me this, why are you on a one-way ticket out of the city?" Kandice wanted to know because she needed to make sure that their business dealings would not come back to bite her in the ass.

"Kontagious, there is no need to worry. The shit I did will not come back on you. I need to leave for personal reasons. In fact, I need to hurry up so I can catch my flight," Lisa said as she stood.

As Kandice stood to hand Lisa the money, Lisa's cell rang. Lisa answered the call and placed the phone to her ear, but didn't speak. The voice on the other end of the phone belonged to her husband, and he said only five words to her before hanging up. "Bitch, I will find you."

Tears of fear fell from Lisa's eyes as she dropped the phone on the floor. She looked at the woman she knew as Kontagious. "I have to leave," she said frantically. "I did my part, now give me my money!" She stuck out her hand and Kandice placed the money in her palm. Lisa flung open the office door and hauled ass out of the store, leaving both Kandice and Marshane wondering what the hell had just happened.

Lisa was in such a rush that she never retrieved her cell phone. Kandice picked up the phone and placed it on her desk. Her curiosity had gotten the best of her. She was going to do some snooping later, but she needed to talk with Marshane first to see what information her employee had been able to gather.

Kandice walked to the front of the store where Marshane was waiting patiently. Marshane pulled out two laptops and booted them up. Once they were both up and running, she asked, "Do you want to see what's popping with the home computer or the office network?"

Kandice thought for a brief second. "The office network," she responded.

Marshane typed in a few things and like magic all of Derrick's office information appeared on the screen. They both took a seat on the stools at the front counter so Marshane could point out to Kandice the documents that might be of interest to her. Marshane and Kandice looked at all of the office files. Kandice was flabbergasted by what she was reading. Her husband had offshore bank accounts, multiple insurance policies, multiple deeds to properties, and it seemed as if he had embezzled money from his clients. But the one thing that caught her eye the most was his list of potential clients. One name in particular was all that she was concerned about—Chance.

On the home computer there wasn't much that she saw that would benefit her in her quest. Marshane downloaded the information from both systems onto two jump drives. After the information was transferred, Kandice sent Marshane home with more instructions. Seeing Chance's name on her husband's potential client list made her wonder how the hell he'd gotten involved with Derrick. The world really was a small place.

Kandice locked up the store and retreated to her office. She wanted to look at the documents Lisa had provided earlier and she didn't want to be interrupted. Kandice took the file out of her purse and began to carefully read each paper. She was trying to concentrate on the papers, but her thoughts kept getting interrupted by the constant ringing of Lisa's cell phone.

After the third time the phone rang, Kandice was frustrated. She picked up the phone and saw that all of the calls were from the same person. She memorized the name, and then turned down the phone's ringer volume. She needed to concentrate on the paperwork before her.

Kandice had come to the part of the file that contained birth records and family information. She pulled out one birth certificate and the information that she read was what she expected, but the second birth certificate almost caused her to faint. There could be no way that what her eyes were reading was the truth! The only words that left her mouth was, "What the fuck!" and "Wow!"

She was so consumed with what she was reading that she did not hear the knocking of someone at the front door of the store. Kandice was still in shock when the ringing of Chance's ringtone on her cell snapped her back to reality. She grabbed the phone and answered.

"Hey, baby! What's up?" she asked as she gathered her thoughts.

"Girl, come open this door! You didn't hear me banging on the glass? Hurry up, 'cause I want to see your beautiful face!" Chance told her as he ended the call.

Kontagious

Kandice picked up the papers that were strewn across her desk. She filed them back inside the folder and placed the folder inside her top desk drawer. She then fixed her lipstick and headed to open the door. When she reached the door she was greeted by her handsome man.

"Hey, boo!" she said as she locked the door behind him and kissed Chance passionately on his luscious lips.

Chance wrapped his arms around her body and their tongues danced for over a minute before they separated. "Damn! You 'bout to make me do something to you, and I ain't come over here for all of that!" he said, laughing as he slapped her on her ass.

The two of them walked back to the office and took seats next to each other. Chance looked stressed, and the last thing she wanted was for him to be stressed. She placed her hand on his face and told him, "You can talk to me. I can tell something is bothering you."

Chance half smiled. He was glad that she was in his life, and even happier that he was getting out of the game. Once he was done with the last bit of work, he was officially done. Chance had never told Kandice details about his business dealings, but what he did tell her was enough for her to read between the lines and understand that his business ventures were illegal.

"Check it, a nigga got a lot on his mind," Chance said as he deeply inhaled and exhaled. Shit has been crazy the last few days. I don't even know where to start."

Kandice wanted him to talk to her so she could make his problems her problems. He didn't know it yet, but she was making plans for him to be the last man standing. She would become his woman, and eventually his wife. They were seven years apart in age, but she was ready to start a family and get Derrick out of her life permanently. She knew that she was wrong for not trying to fix the problems in her marriage, but there was no way in hell she could overlook Derrick's betrayal of their vows. Kandice smiled. She leaned in and kissed his face, trying to reassure him.

Chance sighed and thought about the things that were weighing on his mind. He decided to let Kandice inside his world of problems. He did feel that he could trust her.

"If you want to know what's good, let me start from the beginning. The other day I'm kicking it with my boy Quinton, and we were waiting on J-Rock to come holla at us when J-Rock called, telling us that his wife Alisaya had beat his ass and robbed him, and he needed us to run him to the hospital. Instead of us running him to the emergency room, we went to his crib, picked him up, and took him to my moms, who's a nurse.

"When we got there to get him, we could see that Alisaya had fucked him up! Now don't get me wrong, I done told that nigga J-Rock that he needed to stop putting his hands on his wife 'cause that is some punk shit. I guess she finally snapped and gave him what he was giving her. Since then he's been trying to find her, but it seems she got ghost. Oh, and that reminds me, I want you to come with me to my retirement/real estate venture party tomorrow night.

"I'm ready to get out the game, turn my dirty money into clean money, and hopefully get you away from the lame whose wedding ring you wear. So what's up? You rolling with me or what?" Chance asked as he came to the end of spilling what was on his mind.

Kandice had listened to Chance's story and realized that the world really was entirely too small. After Chance finished revealing his woes, Kandice needed to have some questions answered to confirm the suspicions forming in her mind. If she played her hand right, at the end of the day Derrick would have the shock of his life, and her revenge would be complete. Without giving away the fact that she was trying to get additional information, she decided to ask what was on her mind without coming off as being nosey.

"So, your mom is a nurse?" Kandice asked, hoping that he would say his mom's name when he responded.

Before Chance could answer her, though, the cell phone left by Lisa vibrated. The vibrating of the phone caused them both to look at the desk. Kandice grabbed the phone and placed turned it off. Before, she turned the phone off Kandice looked at the name and number, and saw that once again it was the same person calling.

Apparently Kandice wasn't meant to have her first question answered, let alone any of the other questions she wanted to ask, because after Lisa's phone rang, Chance's cell rang and he suddenly had to run.

"Baby, we gonna have to have this conversation later. I'm going to scoop you up tomorrow night about nine forty-five and you can meet my mom. Make sure you wear something sexy," Chance said before he leaned over and kissed her pouting lips.

Kandice walked Chance to the door, but before she unlocked it she asked, "Will your real estate contact be at the party? I might want to invest some of my money too."

Chance laughed. He loved it when a woman was about her business. He knew right then that he would be able to make major moves with Kandice by his side, and her words only solidified his desire to get out of the game. "Yeah, boo, Alexis will be there. And I should be meeting with her boss in the next few weeks."

The mention of Alexis's name confirmed all that Kandice needed to know. The Chance on Derrick's list was the same person as her Chance. She unlocked the store's door and allowed Chance to exit. She winked and said, "Pick me up from here tomorrow night."

Kontagious

Chance nodded and walked to his car. Kandice watched as he got inside the vehicle. After he pulled off, she walked back inside the store and went back into her office. She immediately took out the file that she'd gotten from Lisa and shook her head. The information that she held in her possession was better than crack to a crackhead.

She had hit the jackpot, and now it was time to get the ball rolling on what she'd been putting into motion for both Derrick and his baby's mother. Thanks to both Marshane and Lisa, she had the rundown on her perceived enemies. And having the 411 gave her the ability to put her nuclear bomb in motion.

CHAPTER 19
Showdown

It's not enough room in this town
For you and me so let's get down
I'm sick and tired of you and this down low fight From
contagious all the way to Mrs. Price
You done it now with Ms. Black Asia
I knew something was funny when she stopped paging
House, cars, shopping mall
Man I tell you it's a battle call
Like a raging bull
I'm about to charge
Kelly, you won't see tomorrow
It's time to put a end to your late night creeps
Now any last words before my pistol speaks...
Showdown... By: R. Kelly

Derrick was working late at his desk when received a text from Kandice asking him to meet her at the Hilton at around two in the morning. The text also said that she had a surprise for him. He read the message and then walked from his office down the hall to Alexis's office. She was putting the finishing touches on the last of her workload.

Derrick knocked on the door and walked in. They both looked at each other with sexual hunger, but they resisted the temptation to fuck in the office, especially since the secretary was still there. Derrick walked to her desk and said, "Tonight's the night for the party. Make sure you scout out any of his friends for the next lick."

Alexis nodded. Derrick had introduced her to his scheme and it was a lucrative venture if they played their cards right. The scheme was not complex. Alexis scoped out potential clients to see how much money they had. The next step was for her to make herself available to the mark. Once the meeting was set, she sold them on the business venture. When the mark's John Hancock was on the dotted line, Derrick took the investment money from the client and placed it in several different accounts. Then Derrick would sell the properties that the client had invested in without telling the client, and Empire Real Estate would keep all the money.

Alexis and Derrick talked a few minutes longer before they said their goodbyes. Alexis headed home to get dressed for the evening. She had a few errands to run before she went to DJ's daycare to pick him up. She had to pick up her outfit from Neiman Marcus, get a quick manicure and pedicure, and get her hair done.

It was almost a quarter to ten before Alexis was dressed for the night. She packed the last of her son's clothes, applied her makeup, and called Derrick to let him know that she was headed out the door. On her way to the club she had to drop DJ off at the babysitter's house. Once she got there she kissed DJ, told him that she loved him, and then finally headed to the party.

Kandice and Chance walked into the club arm-in-arm, looking like a powerful black couple. Chance wore Armani black slacks, a classic white Armani long sleeve shirt, and his black crocodile Gucci loafers. Topping off his outfit was his cross necklace that gleamed brightly as the ten-carats of flawless FL diamonds blinded anyone looking at it.

Kandice was stuntin' herself, shining right along her man. She strutted next to him wearing a black Michael Kors matte one sleeve jersey dress, Christian Louboutin gold alti pump spikes, Michael Kors gold bangles, and Tiffany diamond studs. She had flawlessly applied her MAC makeup, and the fresh coat of clear lip gloss gave her lips the look of luscious silk.

Chance introduced Kandice to J-Rock, Quinton, and a few of his associates. Chance was the guest of honor, and most of the niggas were on his dick, 'cause the woman on his arm was the baddest bitch in the room, hands down. The bottles were flowing, the music was pumping, and everyone was having a good time as they saluted Chance.

"You look beautiful tonight," Chance told Kandice. "I want to introduce you to my moms," he said as he kissed her glossed lips. Kandice smiled at his compliment. She was glad that he liked what he saw when he looked at her. She always felt sexy and appreciated when she was with Chance. She kissed him back, but while their lips were interlocked, Chance suddenly stopped because he felt a hand on his shoulder.

When he turned to see who had interrupted his intimate moment, he saw his mother standing there. He smiled brightly as he placed his arms around her and squeezed her. Since the divorce of his parents, he and his mother had become closer. Although he and his father were still tight, Chance was definitely a mama's boy. Chance talked with his pops a few days prior to the party and he told him that he was coming to town in the next few weeks to see him, but he sent him a gift to commemorate his retirement.

After greeting his mother, Chance turned to properly introduce Kandice to the other important woman in his life. He stepped to the side and let the two women see each other face to face before he said, "Kandice, this is my mother, Charlotte Jackson."

Kandice had just gotten confirmation of another piece of the puzzle when Chance said his mother's full name. Although the pieces that made up this puzzle still amazed her, there was no doubting them now.

Though, her mind was moving at the speed of light she calmed her thoughts down and responded, "It's a pleasure to meet you, Ms. Jackson," Kandice said as she hugged the older woman.

The two women embraced and began talking as if they had always been friends. Chance walked away, allowing them to get acquainted. He saw J-Rock and Quinton on the other side of the room. He looked one last time at the two women in his life and then proceeded over to his boys. When he finally made his way over to them, J-Rock and Quinton were talking about Alisaya. J-Rock was still hot about his ass whooping, and apparently he had still not found his wife.

"Yo, she got to come out of hiding sometime, and when she do, I'ma kill her!" J-Rock said just as Chance approached them.

Chance shook his head when he overheard his boy say that he wanted to do harm to his wife. "Nigga, you dead ass wrong! You done beat that girl's ass so many times, and the one time she beat your ass, you want to kill her!" he said as he sipped his drink.

Kontagious

J-Rock and Quinton both looked at Chance. J-Rock knew how both Chance and Quinton felt about how he physically abused his wife, but it was the only way he knew how to show that he loved her. For J-Rock, beating a woman's ass showed his love. After witnessing his mother being physically abused by his father for many years, he equated hitting a woman with him showing love. Now, that she was gone and he was unable to locate her; he was now reconsidering that his ways was not working for the benefit of his marriage. J-Rock loved his wife, and he hoped that he could change and get his wife back.

"Yo, don't judge me. I know I have my faults, but y'all know I love my wife," J-Rock said. The three friends let the subject drop and continued to mingle and party.

The party was jumping and everyone was having a great time when the DJ got on the mic and asked, "Where is the man of the hour? Where you at, Chance?"

When Quinton and J-Rock heard the DJ shouting out their boy, they raised their glasses and shouted "Here he go!"

The DJ heard their shouts and said over the mic, "Everyone raise your glasses as we salute our man of the hour. We wish you well in your business endeavors."

Glasses were raised to the sky as the guests saluted Chance. Chance smiled and humbly accepted the toast in his honor. He then walked up to the DJ booth and requested that the DJ play Jay-Z's "Excuse Me Miss." When the song came on, he and Kandice's eyes met from across the room. He walked to where she was still talking to his mom and said, "Excuse me, miss, can I have this dance?"

Kandice and his mom both smiled. Kandice kissed Ms. Jackson on the cheek and stepped onto the dance floor with her man. As they danced amongst the other couples, Kandice turned her back to Chance and started grinding her plump ass into his crotch. They were dancing as if they were the only two people on the dance floor.

When the song changed and the sounds of Melanie Fiona's "It Kills Me" blared through the speakers, Chance grabbed Kandice and pulled her close so they could slow grind to her silky voice. Kandice enjoyed being in Chance's arms. She smiled as she listened to him attempting to sing the song in her ear. As she was being serenaded, she felt someone's eyes piercing her.

In true diva fashion she led Chance in a turn as she scanned the room for the eyes that were glued on her. When she spotted who was staring at her, Kandice smiled. The look on Alexis's face was priceless as she watched Kandice and Chance dance like lovers caught up in the rapture of their love.

Kandice had been wondering when Alexis was going to show up, and now she had her answer. She winked, letting Alexis know that she had seen her. The song was coming to an end when Chance and Kandice kissed passionately, only solidifying to Alexis's prying eyes that Kandice was indeed fucking Chance.

Kandice and Chance made their way off the dance floor and over to where J-Rock, Quinton, and Alexis were talking. Chance was happy to see Alexis because he wanted to introduce her to Kandice. Since the day before when Kandice had asked about his real estate connection, he had been thinking of a few ways that together he and Kandice could take the real estate game to another level.

Chance smiled at Alexis and said, "Alexis, this is my girl, Kandice. Kandice, this is Alexis, my real estate connect. Alexis, Kandice is a potential client. She's interested in real estate also."

The two women looked at each other for a moment before Kandice broke the silence between them. "It is my pleasure to meet you, Alexis," she said as she extended her hand.

Alexis plastered a fake smile on her face, shook Kandice's hand, and said, "The pleasure is all mine."

Kandice smiled because she knew Alexis thought she had the upper hand by catching Kandice with the next man, but all along it had been Kandice's plan for Alexis to catch her with Chance.

Kandice kissed Chance on the cheek and said, "Babe, I'm about to head to the ladies' room. Could you get me another glass of champagne? I will be right back."

Right on cue, Alexis said, "I'll go with you so we can discuss business."

Kandice turned and proceeded to walk to the restroom. Alexis followed. They did not say one word to each other as they walked to the ladies' room. Kandice pushed the door to the restroom open and walked inside. She walked to the sink, pulled out her lip gloss, and waited for the showdown to commence.

Kandice applied her lip gloss while Alexis stood to the side and placed her hands on her hips. Kandice continued what she was doing, not even acknowledging Alexis.

"So you gonna fuck around on your husband and have the nerve to be in public with the other man you fucking?" Alexis finally asked. "You are a trifling woman for flaunting your whoring ways for all to see, knowing full well that you're a married woman! Who do you think you are?"

Kontagious

Kandice finished applying her lip gloss, walked to all of the stalls to make sure there was no one in them, and then she locked the bathroom door so no other woman could enter. Kandice finally turned to face Alexis. I am that bitch that has the man you want!" Kandice said as she spoke close to Alexis's face. "Women like you make me fucking sick! You want to come off as if you not guilty. Bitch, you have fucking nerve when not only are you fucking my husband, but you are his baby's mother! Don't worry about what the fuck I do, 'cause, sweetie, I got something for both of y'all! But for the record, you can have my husband, because when I'm done with him, he won't be of any use to me anymore!" With that said, Kandice unlocked the door and exited the bathroom before Alexis had a chance to respond or defend herself.

Alexis looked at the closed bathroom door in with a complete stupid stare. She and Derrick had kept their relationship and child a secret, or so they'd thought. Now Kandice was telling her that she knew the truth about their family. Instead of her feeling bad that she was the mother of another woman's husband's child, Alexis actually felt relieved that the truth was finally out.

"Now he can leave her and be with me and his son," Alexis said as she picked up her cell and started dialing Derrick's number. Although Kandice knew about her and Derrick, she was sure that Derrick did not know about Kandice fucking another man, and Alexis wanted to be the first to tell him.

When the call she had placed was finally answered, Alexis heard a voice that was not Derrick's. The voice on the other end of the line said, "Thank you for calling Kentucky Fried Chicken. How can I help you?" Alexis did not respond. Instead she hung up and pressed the redial on her phone. The same voice picked up again and said the same thing.

Alexis knew that she had dialed the right number, and she could not understand why she was being redirected to KFC. The joke was on her, because knowing that Alexis would try to call Derrick to spill the beans, Kandice had Marshane tap into Alexis's cell phone and change the number she had programmed for Derrick, so that Alexis would be connected with KFC anytime she called Derrick's number. Revealing her infidelity to Derrick was a surprise that Kandice wanted to reveal to Derrick herself.

Alexis dialed the number one final time and met with the same result. She tried to send Derrick a text message, but the text kept coming back to her phone saying that it was undeliverable. Frustrated, she headed back to the party. When she got back to where J-Rock and Quinton were hanging out, she asked where Chance and Kandice had gone.

"You just missed them," Quinton said. "They dipped for the night, but Kandice told us to tell you that it was nice meeting you."

Kontagious

Alexis nodded. She stood there with them and talked for a few minutes before she left, walking to the bar to get herself a drink. As she sipped her drink at the bar, scanning the room full of people, her mind drifted back to her confrontation with Kandice. It had been quite an enlightening night, but little did Alexis know that the real showdown was still to come.

ACT VI

CHAPTER 20
Someone Sleeping in my Bed

I got this feeling, and I just can't turn it loose
That somebody's been getting next to you
I don't want to walk around knowin' I was your fool
'Cuz being the man that I am
I just can't lose my cool
My friends keep telling me about the things that's going
on babe
But deep in my heart baby I hope that I'm wrong
Yes I hope I'm wrong but I know it babe

Somebody's sleeping in my bed, my bed baby
Somebody's takin' my place (baby)
Somebody's sleeping in my bed baby
And you know just what I mean, oh oh oh oh oh!...
In My Bed… By Dru Hill

    Derrick sat in his car in front of Virgil's house at
four in the morning, consumed with rage as he replayed

the events of the last hours in his mind. He had been sitting there for over an hour. He was in such deep thought that he did not hear the click of the loaded .45 when it pressed against his driver's side window.

"Boy, what the hell you doing in front of my house at four in the morning? You 'bout to have your fucking brains blown out on the steering wheel if I hadn't recognized you!" Virgil said as he placed the safety back on the gun, walked around to the passenger door, and got inside the car.

Derrick was so distraught that he was at a loss for words. Virgil sat quietly as he waited for Derrick to speak. He was very close to Derrick and had helped to raise him as if he was his own child. For many years he and Virgie never let Derrick believe anything differently, although Virgil had been thinking lately that it might be time to tell Derrick the whole truth.

As those thoughts traveled through Virgil's mind, Derrick opened his mouth and said, "I should kill that bitch and her nigga!"

Virgil looked at Derrick, trying to determine the context of that comment. Instead of asking him what he was talking about, he waited silently, knowing Derrick would elaborate.

"Man, Kandice is not only scandalous, but she trifling too!" Derrick blurted out.

Kontagious

Virgil saw the anguish on Derrick's face and wanted to hear the rest of the story. But first he wanted a glass of Remy Martin Louis XIII cognac on the rocks.

"Look, I can tell whatever the hell happened between you and Kandice has you vexed. Let's go in the house and talk about it over drinks. The liquor will calm your nerves. Besides, I don't need your black ass going out doing some dumb shit and you catching a charge," Virgil said as he opened the passenger's door and made his way out of the car.

Derrick was still inside the car when Virgil made his way around to the driver's side door. As Virgil looked at Derrick sitting behind the wheel and staring straight ahead, two emotions plagued Virgil—anger and frustration. Derrick's reaction to this situation was unacceptable. Grown men didn't act the way Derrick was acting. They took their disappointments in stride and kept it moving.

Virgil shook his head and opened the driver's side door. "Nigga, if you don't get your love sick ass out this fucking car, we going to have a problem! I know you going through some bullshit right now, but you have to keep your head and approach the situation calmly. Let's go in the house and talk about what's going on."

Derrick finally pulled himself out of the car and followed Virgil inside. Virgil poured their drinks and

Derrick sat down on the plush leather sofa in Virgil's man cave, sipping on his posh Cognac.

Virgil sat behind his executive desk, pulled out one of his Gurkha His Majesty's Reserve cigars, lit it, and took a deep pull. He was now relaxed and ready to hear Derrick's drama.

Derrick looked up, sighed, and took another sip from his glass. He leaned back into the sofa and began to speak.

"The shit was crazy! I walked in on my wife riding the next nigga's dick!"

When Virgil heard that opening statement, he almost choked on the brown liquor that was making its way down his throat. He knew he was in for one hell of a story now. He Virgil didn't know what to say in response, so instead of making the situation worse with an offensive comment, he decided against saying anything at all. He would let Derrick tell him the whole story before putting his two cents in the mix.

Derrick got up from the couch, walked to the center of the floor, and faced Virgil. He took another sip of his drink and let his mind travel back to the scene of the crime—the hotel room.

"Man, the shit was crazy as fuck!" Derrick continued. "I was supposed to be meeting Kandice at the hotel because she said that she had a surprise for me. You know me, I didn't think too much about it. I'm thinking we were about to get into some freaky shit and maybe she had another woman there for me to fuck with her.

"So I texted her and told her that I was on my way there. She didn't respond to my text, but I just chalked that up to her getting ready for me to put down the pipe. I drove there, pulled out the room key that she'd left for me in my car, and walked into the hotel. When I got to the penthouse door, I paused because I heard music coming from the inside of the room.

"In my head I'm like hell yeah! My girl getting the mood right! So before entering the room I unbuckled my belt and undid a few of my shirt's buttons. When I walked in the room it was dark and the music was playing from inside the bedroom. The way the penthouse suite was set up, I had to walk through the living area to get to the bedroom. I walked into the bedroom and saw Kandice on the bed mounted on somebody. My first thought was that she and another chick were doing their thing, and just the thought of this brought a sly smile to my face.

"But those thoughts me and a Ménage à Trois were instantly crushed when I saw a man's hands grab my wife by her waist and pull her down on his dick! I was stuck on stupid for a minute and was in a caught in a hypnotic trance. My words were caught in my throat, and to make the shit worse, Kandice turns her head, and I swear she smirked when she sped up on this nigga's dick and busted all over his dick!

"The dude was so caught up in the rapture of busting his nut that he didn't hear my feet picking up pace toward them. I was stopped in mid stride, though, because three things happened at the same time—dude busted his nut, Kandice reached under the pillow and pulled a gun on me, and ol' boy opened his eyes. The dude was the first one of the three of us to speak when he asked, 'What the fuck is going on, Kandice?'"

Virgil sat on the edge of his seat as he listened to. Although he could understand why Kandice did what she did, she didn't have to let her husband find out that way. That was just downright cold. Virgil took another pull from his cigar and concentrated again on what Derrick was saying.

Derrick went to take another sip from his drink before continuing, and realized it was gone. He walked back over to the bar to refresh his drink, and then continued.

"I looked at the two of them and shouted out to the man who had his dick inside my wife, 'What the fuck you mean what's going on! Nigga, you fucking my wife! That's what's the fuck is up! Kandice, you fucking this nigga, huh!' But as I stepped closer to the bed, I was stopped when Kandice released the safety on the gun.

Kontagious

"Kandice un-mounted the dude and stood butt ass naked before both of us. The dude got up, put on his pants, and stood beside Kandice as she tried to place a robe over her body. Then Kandice decided to open her fucking mouth and add her two cents in the mix. 'You like your surprise?' she asked. 'I thought you would love it! Derrick, meet my other man!'

"When she said that, I lost it! I lunged at her, but the dude stepped in front of her and the two of us collided and fell on the bed. He and I were going at it, getting the best of each other, when out of nowhere Kandice hit me square on my head with the gun. When I grabbed my head, the dude hemmed me up and pinned me to the floor.

"I looked at dude and said, 'You can have that bitch! Just know she is my wife and death will do us part!'

"So Kandice tapped the dude on his shoulder and told him to let me go, and that she would deal with me later. The dude didn't say one word and began to let me up from his grasp. As soon as he did, and I was standing on my feet, I stood directly in front of my wife. I reached back and slapped the dog shit out of her. Then the dude tried to reach for me to hit me again, but I blocked his punch and tackled him, slamming him into the wall.

"We were making so much noise that I guess some of the other guests from the other rooms called security on us. Next thing I know, the door burst open and we were getting bum rushed by the hotel's security squad. They came in like the fucking police, trying to break up the fight between us. When we finally got separated, they asked us to vacate the premises or they would be calling the authorities. Needless to say, I bounced before the shit hit the fan, leaving Kandice and dude in the room to clean up the mess with the hotel."

Derrick took the last sip of his cognac. He looked at Virgil to see what words of wisdom or advice he had to give. When Virgil remained quiet, Derrick walked to the bay window and gazed out into the early morning as the sky began to lighten and indicate the start of a new day. Derrick was actually hurt by his wife fucking another man. Part of him wanted to work it out with his wife, and the other part of him couldn't get past the fact that she had allowed another man inside her secret garden.

Virgil leaned back in his chair and thought about all that Derrick had told him. He was never one to interject himself into other people's intimate relationships, but Derrick had showed up at his doorstep, so now Virgil had been placed in the mix. Virgil lit another cigar and inhaled deeply. His thoughts ran rampant as he searched for the appropriate words to say.

"You can't be too mad with Kandice, especially with your situation," Virgil finally said. "The question is, what do you want to do? I mean, do you still love her?" Derrick thought about Virgil's question. The fact of the matter was that he did have his own foul shit that he needed to account for. To make the situation more complicated, he did still love his wife. With all of the mixed emotions swarming around within him, the only thing that he wanted to do was sleep and hopefully dream his problems away.

"I can't answer those questions at this very moment," Derrick responded. "The only thing I want to do is lie my head on a pillow and try to sort the shit out in my head."

Virgil extinguished his cigar, got up from his chair, and walked toward the doorway of his man cave. Before exiting, he turned around and said, "You know where the guest bedroom is. Make yourself at home for the rest of the morning." He then walked out of the room and retreated to his master bedroom, leaving Derrick to his thoughts.

Derrick continued to look outside, watching the sun rise. He walked to the bar and placed his glass on top of it. The last hours of his life were shattering not only to his emotions, but to his ego. His male ego was bruised beyond repair. Watching another man fucking his wife was one thing in life that he had never prepared for.

Derrick hit the light switch, turning off the light off in the room, and headed up the stairs to the guest bedroom. Once inside, he undressed, leaving on only his Armani boxers. He closed the bedroom door and lay on the king-sized bed. As soon as his head hit the Classic

Down Pillow and he closed his eyes, scenes of the night's events rushed through his mind. He quickly opened his eyes.

He lay there until his eyes could no longer remain open. Derrick finally fell asleep, but his sleep was not a restful one. He tossed and turned until his mind gave into the sleep that his body was calling for. His dreams were nightmares. When he awoke he knew that he and Kandice had unfinished business. The only questions that remained were when and where they were going to finish.

CHAPTER 21
You Think Your Shit Don't Stink

I know you'd like to think your shit don't stank
But lean a little bit closer, see Roses really smell like poo
ooo oop Yeah, roses really smell like poo ooo oop…
Roses… By: OutKast

Kandice was headed home after being out for three straight days. She knew Derrick was going to be at the house waiting for her return, and she was ready for the war that was about to begin. Kandice knew her husband well, and she knew the confrontation between them was about to get physical.

She'd had to convince Chance not to come back with her to the house. He even pleaded with her not to go, telling her that he would replace anything she needed or wanted that was left at the house. But Kandice could not tell Chance that the only reason she was going back to her house was because she was about to shatter her husband's world with the secrets she knew. She had been saving the information for this very moment.

As she drove down the street headed to her house, an evil grin graced her lips, and then a laugh escaped her mouth. Kandice was remembering the look of utter disbelief on Derrick's face when he walked in on his surprise. Just thinking about the scene brought her pure pleasure and satisfaction.

Kandice drove slowly until she reached her house's driveway. She saw Derrick's Bentley parked in the driveway and knew he was waiting on her. As she was opening her car door, the front door opened and Derrick stepped outside. Kandice hesitated, because the last thing she needed was to have this discussion in front of the house for all her nosey neighbors to see.

As she contemplated her options, Derrick headed toward her. Kandice stepped out of her car and placed her feet on the ground. When she closed her driver's side door, the domestic battle popped off.

Derrick and Kandice stood facing each other, neither one of them saying anything, but both of them holding their ground. Kandice looked directly into her husband's eyes and could tell that he had shed some tears in her absence. For a second she felt bad for her infidelity, but as soon as the emotion of guilt entered her soul, it exited when the thought of Derrick's ready-made family flashed through her mind. She sighed before speaking.

"It's over, nigga. I came for some of my things."

When she said those words in such a callous manner, a switch flipped inside of Derrick and his hand reached out and grabbed Kandice by her jct-black, shoulder length hair. He pulled her by her mane and forced her inside their residence. The cries from his wife went unnoticed as he applied more pressure to her head.

He kicked the front door open and flung Kandice inside the house, making her body hit the floor inside the foyer. Derrick stood over her, and he was like the incredible hulk on steroids staring down at her. Kandice scooted backward as he continued to hover over her body.

"Bitch, you better believe this shit is over between us! I don't even know why your funky bitch ass is even here! I should put this size twelve to your face... disrespectful bitch!" Derrick yelled as he stood over the woman to whom he'd chosen to give his last name.

He hadn't even told Alexis about what had popped off three nights ago. He knew if he told her what had happened, he would never hear the end of her nagging about how he should have chosen her and their child over Kandice.

Kandice was on the floor, but she still knew that she was the one who had Derrick where she wanted him. She slowly got up, folded her arms, and stood in front of her husband. She had let him vent his anger, and now it was time to cut the bullshit and tell the truth and nothing but the truth.

"You talk like you fuckin' innocent in this entire situation!" she began. "Nigga, fuck you and what you stand for!" Kandice said as she regained her confidence. She walked closer to Derrick so he could see her eyes as she spoke. "Nigga, you just as guilty! You think I don't know about you and your ready-made family? You thought you were going to fuck your baby's mother and play daddy to your bastard son, and I wouldn't find out about it?"

Before she could speak another word, Derrick snapped. Regardless of how he got his son, DJ was still his heart, and he was not about to let anybody disrespect his seed, not even his scorned wife. Derrick's hands grabbed Kandice around her neck. He began to squeeze, causing her to fight for air. Derrick choked his wife until he saw her eyes roll back inside her head. He released her after finally realizing that if he applied any more pressure, he would be catching a case.

Derrick let Kandice hit the floor hard as his hands let go of her neck. She placed her hand around her neck and mentally thanked God that her shallow breaths were now coming at normal intervals. She looked up at the man who had just tried to take her life, and she finally had confirmation that what she had set into motion was all worth it. Kandice dug into her pants pocket and pulled out some crinkled papers. Kandice started laughing. "Nigga, you think you can kill me? Huh, nigga, do you? Fuck you! You think your shit don't stink? You steady trying to get at me, but you need to be trying to find out why Virgie ain't who you think she is to you, stupid muthafucker!"

The mention of his mother's name caused Derrick to pause. The one woman whom he'd loved unconditionally was being thrown in his face. He looked at his wife and the papers that were in her hand. Derrick assumed that Kandice was holding divorce papers and the mention of his mother was just to provoke him further. Never did he suspect that the papers that were in her possession were more devastating to him than officially dissolving the commitment he had made to Kandice before God, family, and friends.

Kandice had Derrick's full attention and she capitalized on the moment. Seeing that she had the upper hand, she pounced like a lion on its unsuspecting prey She gripped the papers tighter in the palm of her hand, but before she had the opportunity to continue taunting him, she was cut off by Derrick's words.

Derrick cleared his throat and regained control of the rage that was steadily building to its boiling point inside him. He took the bait that his wife was throwing at him and asked, "What the fuck are you talking about I need to find out why Virgie lied to me? Bitch, don't lose your life talking shit about my dead mother!"

Kandice thought his last remark was one for the books and she began to chuckle. It was time to drop the bomb. It was time to shock him and dispel the fallacy of his happy childhood. She opened her mouth and pure malice escaped.

"Nigga, Virgie is not your mother! Matter of fact, your mother abandoned your bitch ass, although she did raise her other child! To make shit worse, she fucked two niggas around the time she got pregnant with you, so all in all, you and your son are the true definition of bastards!"

Before Derrick had the chance to strike Kandice again, she pulled out her .22, released the safety, and pointed it at him. "Give me a fucking reason to pull this trigger!"

Kandice had one hand on the trigger and with her other hand she tossed the papers at her husband's feet. When he bent down to retrieve the documents, Kandice saw the chance to attack the man who had just tried to take her life. She stepped close to her husband's face as he was bent over, and she used her size seven wheat colored Timberland boot to connect with the side of his cheek. The force from the kick stunned Derrick and he fell backward while holding the side of his face. Kandice pounced on him before he could recover, and she proceeded to give him the beating of a lifetime. She had never fought back whenever Derrick felt it necessary to place his hands on her in violence. This time, though, before she made her grand exit, she was going to give him back a piece of his own physical torment.

Kandice raised her hand that held the pistol and connected it with the other side of his face. She struck him several more times before her hand got tired. Although, her hand was tired from swinging the gun, Kandice felt an surge of adrenaline race through her body. She now had the strength to finish fighting Derrick. She then dropped the gun and began connecting with his face, throwing combinations of lefts, rights, and jabs.

In the middle of her onslaught of blows, Derrick was able to block one of her hits, grab her, and throw her off him. He rolled over and saw the gun lying on floor. Derrick and Kandice both realized at the same time that the gun was free.

Kandice moved faster and was able to get to the gun first. Although she now had a deadly weapon in her possession, Derrick still decided to lunge toward his wife and tackle her. In the process of him tackling Kandice, the gun fell backward.

In the midst of the chaos that was taking place inside the house, Chance pulled his Rover into the driveway behind Kandice's car. Although he'd told her that he would let her handle her business with her husband, he knew that Derrick wasn't going to let Kandice walk out without a confrontation. He let thirty minutes pass before he headed to her house. He'd found out where she'd lived by placing a GPS tracker on her car before she'd left his house.

He got out the car and saw that the front door was not completely closed. His Jordans walked anxiously to the door. As he got closer he could hear scuffling coming from inside. The sounds caused him to pick up his pace to a brisk jog. Upon entering the house he placed his hand in the waist of his pants and pulled out his Desert Eagle. When he busted inside he saw Kandice's husband getting the best of her.

Chance rushed to where they were fighting and immediately hit Kandice's husband cold on the back of his dome. He didn't hit him hard enough to knock him out, because he wanted the dude to see his face when he administered an ass whooping.

Derrick quickly grabbed the back of his head and turned to see who had attacked him. When he realized that the man who'd had his dick in his wife was the one who'd administered the blow, Derrick focused his rage on him. He disregarded the fact that the dude had a pistol in his hand and charged full speed.

Chance was never one to back down from a physical alteration, and he was always the type to beat a man with his fist first before ending his life with a bullet. So he dropped his gun and threw a right hook at Derrick when he was close enough to touch.

While the two of them tussled, Kandice was able to recover from the wounds that she'd received and was now back on her feet. She saw the two men fighting, but instead of jumping in, she picked up Chance's Desert Eagle, unlatched the gun's safety, aimed the gun, and pulled the trigger. The bullet hit the wall behind the men, causing a lamp to fall to the floor and shatter into pieces.

The gunshot made both Derrick and Chance stop fighting. Kandice walked over to them. She held the gun with a firm grip in one hand, pointing the barrel at the head of her husband. She used her other hand to grab Chance's shirt and help him up from the floor.

Chance got up while Derrick stared down the barrel of the loaded gun. Once Chance was standing, Kandice placed her other hand on the gun, ensuring that her grip was secure.

The room was silent as each person waited to see what the other one would do. Chance placed his hand on the small of Kandice's back and said, "It's time to go."

Kandice never took her eyes off her husband as she stepped backward toward the door.

Derrick slowly rose from the floor as he saw Kandice retreating toward the door. Kandice stopped. "Nigga, this is only round one! I suggest you get ready, 'cause what I have in store for you and your bitch is going to be epic beyond your wildest dreams! Oh, yeah, don't forget what I said about you and your son being bastards. Seek and ye shall find... blind, dumb, and stupid muthafucker!"

Derrick was fuming as Kandice's words pierced deep into his heart. He watched as Kandice and her secret lover, a man whose name he still did not know, backed up to the front door while Kandice continued to point the gun in his direction.

Kandice and Chance were so busy trying to exit the house that they forgot there was another gun lying on the floor. Derrick watched them and glanced at the .22. Kandice and Chance had finally reached the front door and hauled ass outside to their cars. Derrick was right behind them, bursting through the door while busting off the small caliber gun in their direction

When the sound of gunshots echoed in the air just as Kandice and Chance pushed the automatic starter buttons on their cars, Kandice didn't hesitate. She used her gun to bust back at her husband, causing him to duck to avoid having a bullet hit his body.

Kontagious

Kandice and Chance made it to their cars, but they were unable to get in because Derrick was still firing at them. Kandice continued to fire as she opened her door and then ducked behind it to avoid the bullet that flew by her. She raised her body up slightly above the door, lifted the Desert Eagle, aimed at the top portion of her husband's body, and let off three quick shots. The shots caused Derrick to duck and back up into the house.

Kandice fired three more times, which allowed both her and Chance to get into their cars and peel out of the driveway. As the screeching of both of the cars' tires hit the street, the sounds of police heading toward 2035 Marquee Circle Drive sounded in the distance.

Chance pulled his car into the busy oncoming traffic on the freeway. He looked in his rearview mirror and saw that Kandice was right behind him. He turned on his right turn signal and exited the freeway at the next exit. He drove a quarter mile down the street until he parked his car in the lot behind one of his stores. He got out of his car and waited for Kandice to follow suit.

Kandice pulled in beside Chance's Rover and got out of her car. As soon as her foot hit the pavement, she ran straight into Chance's arms. Chance held her and stroked her disarrayed hair that was wild on her head. After what seemed to be an eternity, Chance asked, "You good?"

Kandice looked at her man, and although she had played a vengeful game of deceit, a game that involved the unsuspecting man whose arms were now wrapped around her, her intention was always to be the last one standing with Chance as the prize at the end of the war.

"I'm good," Kandice responded. "As long as I know you riding with me, I'm good. I'm sorry I got you involved in my personal drama, and I was dead wrong for letting my husband find out about us the way that he did. Forgive me? That was some high school shit on my part."

Chance kissed Kandice on her forehead to reassure her that all was forgiven. He had to concur with her that the tactic she'd used was childish, but all in all he was happy that their relationship was now out in the open.

"Listen, I don't agree with how you went about letting your husband find out about us, but since he knows now, I'm down to ride. I'm down for whatever as long as you keep the shit funky with me," Chance told her as he looked in her eyes.

Kandice felt tears well in her eyes. She was letting her conscience make her feel like shit, because she knew her plotting was wrong as two left shoes. She shook her head from side to side in an effort to shake those feelings. Kandice had no other choice but to let the chips fall where they might land, and by the grace of God, Chance would still be riding in her corner.

Kandice smiled. "I will always keep it real. I'm glad that it's me and you against the world."

Kontagious

They hugged again and made their way inside the store through the back entrance Chance was on the verge of exiting the life and he wanted the transition to go smoothly; but he knew that was just a figment of his imagination. He hoped that his involvement with Kandice was worth the drama that the was sure to ensue.

When they got inside, Kandice excused herself and made her way to the restroom to clean up. She walked into the bathroom, turned on the light, and looked at her reflection in the mirror. She fixed her hair and checked for any bruising on her body. Then Kandice reached inside her Fendi bag and pulled out her cell phone. She pressed the number two on her speed dial list, calling Derrick's cell phone.

Back at the house

Derrick stood outside his house trying his best to rid himself and his residence of the boys in blue. They had arrived on the scene right after the shootout and were asking a hundred and one fucking questions. He was able to convince them that it was a failed robbery and that he had scared off the perpetrators. After thirty minutes of bullshitting them, they finally packed up and dipped. Derrick walked inside his house and walked straight to the bar to pour himself a much needed drink.

He took one sip from his glass when the ringing of his cell caught his attention. Derrick wasn't in the mood for idle chitchat, so he let the phone go to voicemail. As soon as the phone stopped ringing, it started again. This happened two more times, and each time he let it go to voicemail. By the third time, Derrick was pissed. He walked into the foyer where the phone was, picked it up without looking at the caller ID, and asked, "Who the fuck is this?"

As he waited for the other person to respond, he could hear sounds of breathing. Just as he was about to end the call and chop it up as a wrong number, the person on the other line spoke.

When he heard the voice he went from a ten to one hundred on the piss-o-meter. He heard the voice of his wife, and what she said caused him to throw the phone across the room and shatter it into tiny pieces.

The only words that Kandice said before ending the call were, "Die slow, bitch!"

Derrick started to walk back into the den, but stopped to pick up the paperwork that Kandice had left. He then continued into the den and took a seat in one of the chairs. He set his glass on the end table and opened the crumpled papers.

Before reading the information that was before him, he sighed deeply, preparing himself for what he might read.

Back at the store

Kontagious

Kandice had her fun at her husband's expense by playing on his phone, so she gathered her things and headed out of the bathroom. As she walked out into the store, her eyes scanned her surroundings for Chance.

She saw him behind the counter and started to walk the short distance to where he stood. Chance was on his cell phone, and Kandice didn't want to disturb him, so she decided to walk around the store. She saw something that she needed and grabbed it. What she grabbed was a burner cell phone and an unlimited phone card. Kandice pulled out two hundred-dollar bills, placed them in front of Chance on the counter, and turned to walk away.

Kandice had realized that she needed to get rid of her cell phone and go off the grid. Now that she had a new phone, she called Verizon and had them disconnect her line. After that, she activated the burner and got a new phone number. She would have Marshane transfer all her contacts over to the new phone later.

When she was done with the phone situation, Kandice dialed Chance's number and waited for him to answer. Chance was still on the phone when his other line beeped from an unfamiliar number. He put the person he was speaking with on hold and answered the unfamiliar phone call.

"Who this?" he asked.

Kandice busted out laughing at how he answered the phone. After her fit of laughter, she asked, "Is that how your mother taught you to answer the phone?"

Kandice walked to the front of the store and hung up the phone. Chance smiled and clicked back over, telling the person on the other line that he would call him back later. He then stepped from behind the counter and stood in front of Kandice. You like playing on phones, I see! What's up with you calling from a new number?" he asked as he slapped her on the ass.

"You weren't paying me no attention when I paid for the phone and card when you were on the phone running your mouth. This is my new number, so program it in your cell.

I'm cutting ties from the old and starting new." Her statement was only partially true, but in her view there was always 90 percent truth and 10 percent lie to anything anyone said.

The two of them talked for a while longer, then Kandice left, heading out to the mall to splurge on a new wardrobe, courtesy of the stack of cash Chance had placed in her hand along with a spare key to where he laid his head.

Back at the house

Kontagious

Derrick finally opened the papers and began to read what was before him. As his eyes read over each piece of paper, he began to feel tears forming in the corners of his eyes. Paper after paper caused his stomach to feel sicker by the moment.

What lay before him were documents telling him that the woman who had raised him was indeed not his biological mother, but instead his grandmother. He read his birth certificate and saw the name of the woman from whose pussy he was pushed. Each piece of paper showed him that his entire life had been a lie. The person who had been the most important person in his life, the one person whom he'd loved unconditionally, was the one who took a huge lie to her grave.

Flipping through the papers, Derrick came across a picture of a woman. He studied the picture and saw the resemblance between himself and the woman. Derrick knew that he was looking at a picture of the woman who had abandoned him, leaving him to believe that Virgie was his mother. As that information sunk in, Kandice's words replayed over and over in his mind. *You think your shit don't stink.*

Everything Kandice had said was true. He was indeed a bastard. When he realized that the facts were the facts, Derrick was devastated. He sat in the chair for over an hour just thinking. His thoughts touched on many things, but the one thought that kept entering his mind was the question why.

Sitting and thinking caused Derrick's mind to become dark with many different emotions. The longer he sat in that chair, the more obsessive his thoughts became. When he finally got up from where he had been sitting, Derrick was no longer the same man. Not even seeing Kandice fucking another man had affected him the way finding out that his life was a lie had. He needed answers, and he was now on a mission to find the whole truth.

ACT VII

CHAPTER 22
Looking for the Truth

Cause most of ya'll niggas can't deal with the TRUTH
Be hatin when you woman start hit you with the TRUTH
Trying to turn it all around when you know it's the
TRUTH
And you always running away from the TRUTH
You lied til you make yourself think it's the TRUTH
Undress the lie tell what you got TRUTH
Should have been up front and just told the TRUTH
But instead you wanna go and try to hide the TRUTH…
The Truth… By: Truth Hurts

   Derrick was consumed with finding out the truth about his biological mother. He had been locked away in his house for the last week, researching. He'd called his secretary to tell her that he was going to be out, and that Alexis was in charge until he returned. Alexis had been calling him constantly, but he was in no state to entertain her hundred and one questions about what was going on with him.

He had poured over all the documents that he had, went to Virgie's house looking for clues, and was using the Internet to find out as much information as he could. At Virgie's house he was able to find his biological mother's birth certificate. Based on when Virgie had his mother, he calculated that his mother was now in her mid-fifties, so she would have been in her early twenties when she had him.

Derrick sat behind his desk as he eagerly waited for a phone call. His hope was that when he got this call, he would hear good news. He sat in the office of his ten-thousand-square-feet home, alone, contemplating how his life could have turned out differently if he was reared by his mother instead of the woman he now knew was his grandmother.

Then Derrick realized that it didn't matter who had raised him. He was brought up in a home with so much love that he felt guilty for even having those thoughts. Before he could think further, his cell rang. On the second ring he answered.

The conversation was brief. Derrick was pleased that his contact had insightful information about the woman whom he so desperately wanted to track down. He hung up the phone and headed out to meet the person to whom he had just spoken. Derrick walked down his driveway and entered his Bentley. Before he put the car into gear, he looked at himself in the rearview mirror.

What he saw was a man who looked tired, worn down, and unkempt. For a man who was known to have impeccable grooming etiquette, he looked as if he had been to hell and back. Derrick studied his reflection for a moment longer, then thought, *Damn! A nigga look rough as fuck! I've become obsessed with finding a woman who apparently didn't give two fucks about me, but I know if I don't find out, I'll go crazy and my obsession to know will overpower my life.*

Derrick pulled out of his driveway and headed to his meeting. He decided that once he got the information that he was paying for, he would clean up and get back to being more of the man he was before he found out the truth about his life.

CHAPTER 23
Stalker

Every breath you take
Every move you make
Every bond you break
Every step you take
I'll be watching you
Every single day
Every word you say
Every game you play
Every night you stay I'll be watching you...
Every Breath You Take... By: Sting

Since Derrick had met with his private investigator, he had obtained a wealth of information about his mother. He now had pictures, additional documents, a place of employment, home address, her second child's birth certificate, a marriage license, and her so-called ex-husband's current prison location.

Derrick was on a mission, and as his mission became clearer, the more demented he became. He was formulating a plan, but for his plan to be fully implemented, he needed Alexis's help. Derrick had called Alexis and asked her to drive him around. Just as Derrick had suspected, she didn't question his motives, but played her position as always. He sat in a raggedy Ford Taurus that Virgil had gotten for him as he waited on Alexis to exit her building.

Alexis finished dressing and was putting on her Nike tennis shoes when Derrick texted her, letting her know that he was waiting downstairs. She was still in the dark about whatever was going on with Derrick, but she was hoping that today she would finally get some answers. Each time she had called him to see what was going on, Derrick had sent her straight to voicemail. After the third day of being sent to voicemail, Alexis got frustrated and stopped calling. She wanted to go to his house, but she didn't want to run into Kandice since their encounter at the club, so she had waited, hoping Derrick would eventually call her.

Alexis grabbed her purse and keys, and headed out the door. When she walked into the parking lot she didn't see Derrick's Bentley. It wasn't until she heard her name being called that she realized that Derrick was driving a hooptie.

She strolled over to the Taurus as Derrick got out of the driver's side and walked over to the passenger's side. Alexis got in the car behind the wheel. As she adjusted the car's settings to her liking, Derrick said, "I need you to drive to this address and wait there until I see who I'm looking for. Then I want you to tail that person without being noticed." He then handed her a crumpled piece of paper with the address written on it.

Alexis looked at Derrick as she extended her hand for the paper. She read the address and saw that it was on the other side of town. Alexis didn't ask any questions, but cranked up the car and pulled out of the parking spot, heading toward the expressway. She made a right onto the freeway and headed north.

The usual fifteen-minute drive ended up taking thirty minutes because of the heavy flow of traffic. After she maneuvered through the traffic, Alexis pulled into the sub-division and drove down the street until she parked the car across from the address on the paper. She and Derrick sat in the car for what seemed like an entirety until Derrick sat up in his seat as his eyes followed a woman exiting the house and getting into a silver two-seater Jag. He looked at Alexis and told her, "Follow the woman in the Jag."

Again Alexis didn't ask any questions. She just did as she was told. She almost lost the woman when she reached the main street leading out of the sub-division, but was able to keep her in view as she followed the Jag from two cars behind.

Derrick watched the silver Jag move through the traffic, turn into the hospital entrance, and head to the employee parking garage. He sat in the car in anxious anticipation as Alexis busted a U-turn because they would not be able to gain entrance into the employee garage without the proper key card. As Alexis placed the car into park, Derrick hoped that the woman would walk inside the hospital through the main doorway that was in view of their car versus going inside through the garage.

Alexis was now ready to ask what the hell was going on. She had followed a woman to the hospital. Her curiosity was beyond piqued. She turned to Derrick and saw concentration etched on his face. She needed to know what he had gotten her involved in.

"What's up, Derrick? Why are we following this woman, and who is she to you?" Alexis finally asked.

Derrick wished that Alexis wouldn't ask questions, but he knew they were bound to come. He wasn't ready to let her in on what was transpiring in his life. However, he knew if he didn't say something, she would continue to ask.

"Look, it's some shit popping off with me right now, and I'm not ready to inform you of what's going on," he responded. "I just need for you to ride this out and play your position."

When Alexis heard Derrick's response to her questions, she became heated. All at once so many things went through her mind. She had been riding with this nigga since he was sixteen and she was eighteen. In all her years of dealing with Derrick, Alexis had always played her position. She played the background even to the point of him marrying another woman, leaving her to raise their child primarily by herself with him playing daddy from afar.

She had had enough of being made to feel as if she was nothing more than a pawn to whatever game Derrick was playing. She quickly turned her body so that she was directly facing Derrick. "Nigga, fuck you! I have been riding with you since before you were who you are now! And to think that I was upset that Kandice found out about us, but I am more than happy that she knows now! Maybe now you will do right by me and DJ, but I think I'm going to pass on trying to be your number one. Let her deal with you and your bullshit! I'm done!" Alexis said as she reached inside her purse for her cell so she could call a cab.

Derrick grabbed Alexis's arm because he could not believe what he had just heard. She knew that Kandice knew about them? What the hell was really going on? Derrick was about to address what he'd just heard, but was cut short when the distinct ringtone for his PI blared from his cell phone.

He had been waiting on this call, because the PI literally held the key to steps two and three of his stalking mission. After he ended the conversation with the PI, he looked at Alexis and said, "We will finish this shit later. I need you to take this car to Virgil. He'll take care of the car and get you to where you need to be. Right now I have to take care of something. This shit ain't over between us!" He placed his hand on the door handle, opened the door, and started walking toward the main street as he made a call on his cell phone.

Alexis was left in the car looking dumbfounded. Once again she was left in the dark without a reason. She had no idea what she had gotten involved in or what the hell was going on. But Alexis had no choice except to comply with what was asked of her. She felt if she did not do right by Derrick that there would never be a chance for she and him to be a family with their son. She felt as if she was trapped between a rock and a hard place. Without any further hesitation, she started the car and pulled off. As she began to leave the hospital grounds she was unaware of the eyes that watched her. The woman she had followed was well aware of the people trailing her, and in an effort to detour them, she led them to the hospital employee garage because she knew they could not get in without a key to the gate.

The woman had been standing at the opening of the gate watching the two people in the car. She knew that she couldn't go back to her house for a second because they knew where she laid her head, so she waited another twenty minutes before she got back in her car and made her exit. The question that raced through the woman's mind was… why was she being stalked?

CHAPTER 24
Plotting

That's not all, MC's have the gall
To pray and pray for my downfall
Pray and pray for my downfall
Pray and pray for my downfall…
My Downfall By: NOTORIOUS B.I.G

Marshane sat at her desk inside what she called her lab. She was putting the finishing touches on her job for Kandice. She was extremely proud of her handiwork. Her fingers typed a few different passwords into the system as she tried to hack into the Child Protective Services employee records. On her last attempt the computer's home screen popped up, saying welcome.

Kontagious

Marshane sighed and got up from her seat. As she stretched her arms above her head, she said, "Damn, I'm good! If this shit goes down the way I know it will, Kandice's husband and this chick 'bout to be in for the shocks of their lives. I actually feel bad for them, because they have no idea what's going on behind the scenes."

Marshane sat back down at her workstation and searched through the CPS employees' files until she came across a name that she liked. She clicked on the name and began to look into the person's case files. The more she looked at the person's workload, the more she liked the person for what she was about to do.

Before she completed this task, Marshane looked at the list of things that Kandice wanted done. She verified that she had completed everything, and this was the last project on the list.

Marshane pulled up one of the cases and read it over. After thoroughly examining the paperwork, Marshane was satisfied that she had found what she was looking for, so she began to work on her last assignment.

***

While Marshane was doing her thing on one side of town, Kandice was getting prepared for the last battle of the war on the other side of town. She looked over each document that was in her possession and she was beyond pleased. As she began to smile at what she had done, she heard Chance coming through the door. Kandice quickly put all of her evidence inside her purse and walked to the front of the house to greet her man.

When she made it to the front of the house, before she could even say hello, Kandice had to make a beeline for the hallway bathroom. She lowered her head to the toilet just as she began to throw up. Chance saw Kandice running to the bathroom and he followed her to make sure that she was all right. When he got to the bathroom he saw her praying to the porcelain god.

"Kandice, baby, are you all right?" he asked as he brushed his hand across her face.

When his hand touched the side of her face, he became alarmed and placed his hand on her forehead. Before he could say that she felt hot, Kandice passed out and collapsed into his chest. Chance was frantic and began to shout and throw water on Kandice's face, trying to wake her.

"Kandice, Kandice, baby, wake up!"

Kandice's eyelids started fluttering but she couldn't keep them open. Chance knew something was wrong and he needed professional help. He picked her up and hauled ass out the front door. He got her inside his truck and pulled off, doing almost ninety to the hospital. He continued talking to her and prayed to God that she was

OK. He would be devastated if he lost her when he'd just gotten her in his life.

By the grace of God he was not pulled over by the boys in blue. After he pulled into the emergency lane of the hospital, Chance put the Range in park, jumped out, ran to the back of the truck, and pulled out Kandice. He carried her inside, calling for help.

When he burst through the doors he was greeted by a nurse who asked what was wrong, but when she saw the face of the woman he held, she gasped with fear. She immediately called for a stretcher and a team to assist her. When Kandice was placed on the stretcher, the nurse said, "Kandice, baby, it's going to be all right!"

Chance was confused as to how the nurse knew Kandice, but he was grateful that she was there. He asked if he could go back there with her. The nurse said no, but she said she would personally come and get him as soon as she knew what was going on. Chance went to move the car away from the emergency entrance and then returned to the waiting area. He was a nervous wreck and wanted to call someone, but decided against that until he knew what was going on. Chance paced with nervous anticipation. He had walked to the nurses' station more times than he could count. He looked at his Blacpain L-Evolution Watch and saw that he had been there almost two hours and there was still no word on Kandice's condition.

Chance was headed back up to the nurses' station when the nurse who'd greeted them when they'd arrived walked up to him. He stopped in his tracks when he saw her coming. The nurse stood beside him and extended her hand for him to shake. They shook hands and then Chance asked, "What's going on? Is she OK? Please tell me what's going on!"

The nurse smiled and introduced herself. "My name is Monica, and Kandice and I are best friends. I can't tell you her condition because you are not family. If you don't mind me asking, why did you bring her here and not her husband?"

Monica was in the ER part of the hospital to check on one of the newborns that was brought in earlier when she saw the man bringing in Kandice. Although, Kandice was awake in the room, Monica didn't ask her about the man who was with her because she was far to nosy for that… she wanted to ask the man for herself.

Chance was pissed because Monica wouldn't provide him with any information, and then to make matters worse, she was being fucking nosey. But he refused to show his ass. Instead he asked, "Can I see her? I need to see her!"

Monica saw that she was not about to get any answers from this man. She knew that she and Kandice were going to have to talk. Without acknowledging

Chance's request, Monica turned around and gestured for Chance to follow her.

Chance walked behind her as they took a series of turns until they arrived at room number 122. Monica walked inside the room with Chance right behind her. When Chance saw Kandice lying in the bed, he brushed past Monica to stand next to her.

"Can you give us a minute?" Chance asked Monica, requesting some privacy.

Monica was not willing to leave at Chance's request, so she walked to the bed and looked at her friend. "Kandice, do you want me to leave you with him?" she asked.

When Chance heard Monica ask Kandice that question as if he was about to hurt her, he could no longer contain his emotions. He snapped his head in Monica's direction. "What the fuck is that supposed to mean?" he asked. "You better walk out that door before the question becomes whether you want to remain in the room with me. Kandice is fine with me!"

Before the bickering could continue and escalate to a full blown verbal altercation, Kandice cleared her throat and said, "Monica, it's OK. Just give us a few minutes."

Chance and Monica stared each other down as Monica walked to the door and exited, closing it behind her. Once the door was shut, Chance let out a loud sigh and sat in the chair next to the bed. He grabbed Kandice's hand and smiled at the woman whom he'd decided to make his number one.

Kandice smiled and sat up in bed. At the moment her thoughts were running rampant, and she was mentally collecting them. She squeezed Chance's hand and said, "I have something to tell you. I hope what I am about to say will make you happy, but if it doesn't, we can talk about what to do."

Chance waited patiently for whatever news she was about to spring on him. He stroked her hair, giving her the reassurance that she could talk to him. In the midst of him stroking her hair, he leaned over and kissed her lips, placing his tongue inside her mouth.

As Kandice prepared to tell Chance what was going on, Monica was dialing Derrick's number. She knew that she was overstepping her boundaries, but in her mind, Monica thought that she was doing the right thing.

Monica walked further away from the other people that were close to her in an attempt to have a private conversation. She was on the verge of hanging up when Derrick picked up. They both said hello at the same time, but Monica wasn't calling for idle chitchat, so she got straight to the point.

Kontagious

As Monica began to speak, Charlotte saw Monica. She began to walk over to where she was, and as she approached, Charlotte heard the tail end of Monica's phone conversation. What she heard almost made her lose her balance.

"Yeah, Kandice is here with some dude...   I think his name is Chance," Monica said. "But what I really wanted to tell you was that she was brought in because she fainted. She's pregnant."

Just as Charlotte heard that announcement, her cell phone began to ring. She looked at the screen and saw Chance's name appear so she answered. Before she could get the hello out of her mouth, her son shouted through the phone, "Mom, you about to be a nana!"

Monica, hearing Chance's loud announcement, turned to see Charlotte standing beside her. Their eyes locked. Charlotte couldn't even enjoy the moment of learning she would be a grandmother, because when she looked into Monica's eyes, her maternal instincts kicked in, alerting her that fuckery was going down, and Monica was the culprit behind the madness.

Finally Charlotte responded to her son's announcement. "Chance, what room are you in? Room 122? OK, I'm on my way up."

When Monica heard Charlotte repeat room 122, she knew then that she had fucked up, because apparently

Charlotte had heard her conversation with Derrick and put two and two together. The two women looked at each other without saying a word, but Monica knew that she was caught in some bullshit, and the only thing she could say was, "Fuck!"

As Kandice lay in the hospital bed waiting for the doctor to release her, she smiled. She had just told Chance why she had passed out, and to her surprise and relief, he was happy about her pregnancy. As for Kandice, she had mixed feelings about being pregnant. She had two dilemmas. The first dilemma was figuring out who was the father of her child—her husband or Chance. Her second dilemma was about all her scheming and plotting to achieve her husband's downfall. Now that she had a child to think about, everything was up in the wind. If Derrick was the father, she wanted him to be in her baby's life, and that wouldn't happen if Kandice continued with her plans of revenge.

As these thoughts raced through her mind, there was a knock at the door and in walked Charlotte. When she walked in she bypassed her son and walked straight to where Kandice lay in the bed. She stood next to the bed and without hesitation said, "Kandice, what type of shit do you have my son mixed up in, and why the hell is Monica telling someone that you are pregnant before you even have the chance to tell it yourself?"

Kontagious

Kandice and Chance were both caught off guard by what Charlotte had said. Before Kandice could close her mouth because of the shock, in walked Derrick and Monica. The room was still as everyone looked at each other, but Derrick broke the silence and asked, "Are you pregnant with this nigga's baby?!!!!"

THE SAGA CONTINUES

ALSO AVAILABLE FROM DIAMOND STONE PRODUCTIONS

A wise man once said, "do your dirt by your lonesome." These are the truest words ever spoke, because when you play the game of money over everything, death before dishonor, hear no evil/ see no evil, and snitches die a coward's death... these are the only rules that apply when you are knee deep in the game.

Too-Reel is both well-respected and feared in the streets of New York, but when he his forced to choose between staying true to his street moral code or risk the freedom of his mother, he is placed in the dilemma of his lifetime.

As Too-Reel stalls for time from both the crooked District Attorney Jerol Highmon and dirty federal agents, he is exposed to how the game has truly been played. Will Too-reel make it out with his dignity or fall victim to the federal government's tactics? In a the game of chess one must out think his opponent and think ten steps ahead... will Too-Reel be able to out think his enemies or will his enemies check-mate him?

DiamondStone Productions is proud to introduce FACE to the world of Urban Lit. Readers and fans alike will know why we are ecstatic about him being an addition to the DSP family.

#JOINTHEDSPTAKEOVER#   diamondstoneoproductions.net

ALSO AVAILABLE FROM
DIAMONDSTONE PRODUCTIONS

A man is supposed to take care of his home, but when the chips are stacked and there's a bitchy wife and the babies need to be fed... a man will do what he thought he would never do for the survival of his family...

Against all odds Charles Profit drifts head first deep into the underworld. He becomes so engaged in his diabolical duties that he totally forgets about the everyday life that he once lived. His deceitful behavior causes his wife Ashley to once again fall victim to her ways that he never knew of. Before they both get a grip on reality, Ashley is head over heels for a drug dealer named P.M. and Charles is clearly at a point of no return.

The action is fast, the situations are real and in no time their deadly game of picket fences that they chose to play leaves them faced with unknown circumstances. The only thing left from there is a small fraction of time for redemption.

ALSO AVAILABLE FROM DIAMONDSTONE
PRODUCTIONS

BEHOLD, A TALE OF TWO EVILS...

Life in the in the criminal underground is threatened by a conglomerate of wolves dressed in sheep's clothing, who uphold justice by day and corruption by night.

Follow closely as those distinguished chameleons target three not-so-innocent victims who become entangled in a deceptive web, where there are no rules except theirs... with two sides in vast world of crime the streets of Hartford, will never be safe when those who control the law-are the same ones who break it...

#JOINTHEDSPTAKEOVER# diamondstoneproductions.net

ALSO AVAILABLE FROM DIAMONDSTONE PRODUCTIONS

BRUISED, battered and set on Revenge!!!

Vasthai was brutally raped at the tender age of sixteen and was a mother nine months later. After putting her life back together with the help of her husband... she is devastated when her son, Tyrone is sent to prison for the same crime as his biological father... rape.

RIDE with Vasthai as she masterminds the ultimate downfall of the man who took her innocence.

Everything you think you know... Is not what it seems!!! "Vengeance is mine said the lord"... That only applies when you... have everything to lose and nothing to gain... But when you have everything to gain... you will take vengeance into your own hands!!!

Once again, NIKKI URBAN has written another urban erotica classic... DAMAGED GOODS is a pager turner, with an out of the box plot.

#JOINTHEDSPTAKEOVER# diamondstoneproductions.net

ALSO AVAILABLE FROM
DIAMONDSTONE PRODUCTIONS

Jade's Diary is a tale of a dead woman's diary that is left to her daughter Mikleah. As Mikleah reads her mother's diary she turns the pages of her mother's secret life that includes sex, lust, lies, betrayal and vengeance.

Mikleah learns from her mother's diary of the father she never knew and of a long lost sibling. Mikleah, Jade's daughter finds out that she has been having an incest filled relationship with the sister that she never knew and learns to what extent her mother would go through to get what she wanted-her lover's wife.

The diary exposes the many secrets of Jade's lovers. These secrets lead to death and imprisonment. Jade's Diary takes you through the lives of Jade's lovers and shows you the Tru definition of a woman's Scorn!!!

#JOINTHEDSPTAKEOVER# diamondstoneproductions.net

DiamondStone Productions LLC
P.O. BOX 11266
Jacksonville, FL 32239
www.diamondstoneproductions.net

NAME: _____

INMATE ID: _____

ADDRESS: _____

_____

CITY/STATE/ZIP: _____

QUANTITY	TITLE	PRICE
	JADE'S DIARY-NIKKI URBAN	$12.00
	DAMAGED GOODS-NIKKI URBAN	$12.00
	HALFWAY CROOKZ- $PAID	$12.00
	THE FACTOR- FACE	$12.00
	PICKET FENCES -WADE	$12.00

SUB TOTAL: $ _____
SHIPPING/HANDLING (VIA US POSTAL SERVICE)
$2.95 PER TITLE
4 OR MORE TITLES- FREE SHIPPING
SHIPPING: $ _____
TOTAL ENCLOSED: $ _____
FORMS OF PAYMENTS:
CERTIFIED CHECKS OR MONEY ORDERS, ALL MAIL-IN ORDERS TAKE
7-10 BUSINESS DAYS TO BE DELIVERED. BOOKS CAN ALSO BE
PURCHASED AT OUR WEBSITE: DIAMONDSTONEPRODUCTIONS.NET
INCARCERATED READERS RECEIVE A $4.00 DISCOUNT PER TITLE.
PLEASE PAY $8.00 PER BOOK PLUS APPLICABLE SHIPPING.